SEX ROMP GONE WRONG

SEX ROMP GONE WRØNG

STORIES BY

Julia Ridley Smith

— BLAIR —

Printed in the United States of America
Cover design by Jason Heuer
Interior design by April Leidig

Blair is an imprint of Carolina Wren Press.

*The mission of Blair/Carolina Wren Press is to seek out, nurture, and
promote literary work by new and underrepresented writers.*

We gratefully acknowledge the ongoing support of general operations by the
Durham Arts Council's United Arts Fund and the North Carolina Arts Council.

Library of Congress Cataloging-in-Publication Data
Names: Smith, Julia Ridley, author.
Title: Sex romp gone wrong : stories / by Julia Ridley Smith.
Description: Durham : Blair, 2024.
Identifiers: LCCN 2023018395 (print) | LCCN 2023018396 (ebook) |
ISBN 9781958888117 (paperback) | ISBN 9781958888131 (ebook)
Subjects: LCGFT: Short stories.
Classification: LCC PS3619.M58878 S49 2024 (print) | LCC PS3619.M58878 (ebook) |
DDC 813/.6—dc23/eng/20230608
LC record available at https://lccn.loc.gov/2023018395
LC ebook record available at https://lccn.loc.gov/2023018396

For Glenn

Contents

Don't Breathe,
Breathe

LEFT FOR THE BEACH straight from the mammography studio. Wrong word, *studio*, but that's what came out as I composed a departing text to the girls. I didn't bother to correct it. Hadn't I just been having my picture taken?

It was a routine mammogram, my first. The technician said, "You're forty-six? And this is your first time? We really like our ladies to start at forty. But it's good you're here now."

I tried not to resent the scolding. It's true, it's a fault of mine—I tend to delay anything unpleasant. The tech directed me to stand next to a giant tan machine that looked scary, boring, and overpriced, like a lawyer or a banker. She said to lower the blue drape off my left shoulder, then put my left arm around the machine, as though I were going to dance with it. She lifted my left breast onto a little plastic shelf, mushed it around, and lowered part of the machine to flatten it. I must've flinched because she said, "Sorry," before going back to her computer station.

She clicked her mouse a few times, mentioning a sale at Macy's. I commented on the heat outside. We talked as two people do when one has the job of shoving the other's private part into a vise, and the owner of the private part is pretending not to mind. In fact I did mind: the skin above my breast felt stretched almost to the point of tearing, and the pressure on the breast itself was cruel. Still, I've had two children, I've known worse pain. Mainly I felt ridiculous. A drape should be classical; off-the-shoulder should be sexy. My cheek pressed against the cold metal, and I kept straining my eye downward, trying to glimpse the pinkish doughy blob mashed under clear plastic. I thought of preparing my daughters' favorite chicken. Throw a split breast in a baggie, pound the shit out of it, fry it in butter.

Instead of saying *smile*, the tech said, "Don't breathe."

Part of the machine moved in a slow humming arc over my clamped breast. I stared at the stock photo of a beached sunset until it finished.

"Breathe."

She clicked a few more pictures, and we repeated the whole rigamarole on the other side.

"Don't breathe...breathe."

Halfway through the drive down to Oak Island, the radio disintegrated into nothing but static and Jesus. Out the window: pine trees forever and signs beseeching me to pull over for Silver Queen corn, South Carolina peaches, cheap gas, and/or eternal life in HIM. I palpated each breast and tried to guess whether the technician had seemed pitying when she told me to expect results in a week. There was no particular reason to worry, but I was going to do it anyway—that's just how I am.

It was early September 2019. My friend Amy had invited me and a bunch of other women to her new five-bedroom oceanfront house at Oak Island, North Carolina, to celebrate her fiftieth birthday. She and I were teachers' aides together in a primary school in the late 1990s. We didn't last there; neither of us really liked working around children. Later, we reconnected at a postnatal yoga class. I'd just had my eldest; she, her youngest of three. Her in Lululemon, me in sweats and an AIDS walk t-shirt. We were the ones giggling when the instructor recommended we envision a healing light in our recovering wombs. Since those days, Amy's inherited a pot of money, orchestrated a lucrative divorce, and built a successful party-planning business that caters to people even richer than her.

The whole trip, I kept poking at my chest. I know the technician can't divulge anything, since she's not a radiologist, but I bet she knows a big ball of cancer when it appears on her screen.

My best friend once asked what I saw in Amy, thinking she must be stupid and shallow because she's tall and blond and fit and showy. On the surface Amy resembles the sort of untrustworthy women that movies and high school taught us to avoid. But the fact is, Amy is smart. Not only does she laugh at my jokes, but she can be pretty funny herself. When you need help, she shows up with her SUV loaded with supplies and doesn't stop until there's nothing left to do. Plus, now she has a beach house, a birthday gift she bought for herself because, as she keeps telling everyone, she's worked hard, she *deserves* it.

Crossing the bridge over the Intracoastal Waterway this time, I barely registered the inner leap of happiness I usually feel at seeing that sparkling band of water. My poor children, if I had cancer. Oh Jesus. After they paid to bury me, they'd have about twelve cents left. Their father has money but good luck getting it out of him.

My phone directed me to a yellow oceanfront behemoth on stilts. Amy wanted to name the house—already had a sign painter lined up—but she hadn't decided what to call it yet. Surely she'd help the girls if I was sick. I pulled in behind her SUV and lugged my bags up the steps. The wraparound porch was Instagram-ready: white rockers, potted plants, and a swinging bed covered with lavender and lime batik pillows.

When my daughters saw the listing on Airbnb, the fourteen-year-old said, "White people be like 'don't you just hate vacuuming all that sand?'"

The seventeen-year-old said, "That is *such* a juvenile expression of your nascent understanding of the construct of race. But also funny."

I suggested (not for the first time) that attempting to combat stereotypes about one group with stereotypes about another group might not be the most constructive approach to social ills.

Child Younger told me to lighten up.

"It's a meme, Mom. It'll say, 'White people be like'... and then it shows a guy who's a really bad dancer."

"But *you're* white. Do white kids send these memes? You send them? Are you supposed to?"

"Oh my god, it's a joke! Why do you have to turn everything into a thing?" said Younger.

"Everything IS a thing," said Child Elder, who at that very moment was drafting a petition to the World Meteorological Organization to make hurricane names gender neutral. As I packed, she warned me that a tropical storm lurked hundreds of miles off the coast of North

Carolina and I ought to keep an eye on the weather while I was at the beach.

"They're already calling it Fernando," she said.

The girls debated whether that was okay, given the troubles at the border and the president's criminalization of Mexicans. They're constantly grappling with the big topics now, asking questions nobody can answer, clamoring for what ought to be, if we lived in a good world. They get so worked up, glaring at me as if I've personally betrayed them, as if I don't want a better world, too, and the shittiness of the current one is all down to me.

"Maybe it's an achievement that we now have weather events with Hispanic names?" said Child Younger. "Did anybody think of that?"

"Latinx," Child Elder corrected. "Or is it maybe an insult? Giving a destructive storm a Latinx name?"

"I think it's actually Fernand," I said.

Both girls stared at me. Younger is always offended; Elder always frets that she's offending. I don't know who to worry about more.

"The storm," I said. "It's going to be called Fernand, I think, not Fernando. I believe Fernand is French or German, maybe, not Spanish."

"Whatever," Child Younger shrugged. Then she looked at me. "They should name a hurricane after you."

"Hurricane Delia," said Child Elder, trying it out.

"You really think I could be a hurricane?"

"Oh, yeah," the baby said. "The way you yell? Category 5. If you wanted to be."

They both thought that was hilarious.

THE FIRST EVENING at the beach passed pretty much the way you might expect when fourteen middle-aged, mostly white, mostly straight, mostly affluent women congregate without men or children in a beach house that rents for $6,500 a week in high season. Amy wasn't charging us, though, because we were her guests. The only guests I knew well were Maeve, who's a caterer and often works with Amy, and Maeve's wife, Sharon, who I used to exchange snarky asides with during PTA meetings at our kids' elementary school.

Amy swore I'd like everybody she invited, and I wanted to think that individually they were probably fine. But as a collection, they intimidated me, with their expensive clothes and casual allusions to pricey trips and cosmetic procedures.

"*You're* Delia?" they said. They'd expected Amy's kooky friend Delia to have purple hair and visible tattoos. What was it I did again? Well, I'd done a lot of part-time jobs after I'd had my children and quit teaching. Now I was mostly making WordPress websites for people, like Amy, and Maeve, and Sharon, who didn't want to pay a professional designer.

"How'd you learn to do that?" one of them asked skeptically.

"I just kind of taught myself?"

Already they were bored with me. Feeling mutual. I stuck to the gleaming kitchen, helping Maeve and another woman cook the spread for Night 1. Maeve is intense. She makes you work, but when it's all finished, you feel so proud of yourself. We made guacamole and hummus, grilled fish, dirty rice, green beans, salad, and peach cobbler and homemade ice cream. Bottles lined the countertop like warheads—white, pink, red; vodka, gin, bourbon—a liquid arsenal against the onslaught of age. We set the oversized table next to a two-story wall of windows that afforded a panoramic ocean view. I wondered how Amy kept the glass so clean and clear despite the salt air always spraying in. Her competence truly is pathological. If I did have cancer, I'd call her right away. I'd have second opinions and wigs and casseroles and a housecleaner and magic vitamins before I knew what hit me.

We feasted like we'd never heard of diets or eating disorders, fat or cholesterol. Then we danced to songs popular so long ago that they'd already circled around to popularity a second time and been forgotten again. People strolled on the beach and lazed in the hot tub. Four snuck off in the dark to get high. Two went to bed early. Two were caught smoking cigarettes, apologized for being gross, then had to share the cigarettes. I was beginning to see who I might like and who I already couldn't stand.

The group consumed a shocking amount of booze, but nobody vomited. Nobody cried. That would be Night 3, and we weren't there yet. Night 1, we were fresh and celebratory. The group cataloged joys. One new grandmother, two divorces (including mine), three career changes, four empty nests, five years sober. A fabulous weight loss story. A cancer remission.

"We are in our fucking prime," said Maeve. "I don't care what anybody says."

"*You* are in your fucking prime," said Sharon, kissing her neck.

Day 2, we planted ourselves in the sand: a garden of yellow and blue umbrellas shading an undergrowth of pastel t-shirts, cheery towels, dizzy kaftans. Only Maeve didn't join us—she never suns herself. Night 2 we took over a restaurant in the town and got a little rowdy. We flirted with the hostess, the waiters, the bartender, the breadbasket, a few other customers, and the baby at the next table. We left a big tip, just in case we weren't as cute as we thought we were.

Day 3, it rained. Half the house slept late. Sharon made extra coffee and texted with her kids. Amy repaired the switch on a lamp, then did sudoku. I painted my toenails and read about how trees basically talk to each other by emitting chemicals through their roots. Jenny (Amy's high school BFF) sorted shells she'd picked up. She only wanted whole ones. Maeve dumped out a thousand-piece puzzle on a card table and worked at it like it was a job. She'd gotten up at six and made a mountain of sandwiches and brownies and herbal iced tea. We could help ourselves whenever.

One by one, the others straggled out of bed. The rain continued, dimpling the gray ocean. There was Ping-Pong in the playroom, reading of paperbacks. We got so bored we decided to watch the movie *Splash.*

As soon as the credits started rolling, Amy said, "And with that, ladies, I announce my retirement, effective immediately, to the owner's suite. I'm going to break in the new vibrator Sharon gave me for my birthday. Thank you, Sharon."

"Mazel tov, my friend."

Off she went.

"Did *Splash* just make Amy horny?" I asked.

"Mermaids are sexy," Sharon said.

Jenny said, "I always wondered why sailors in movies are so hot for mermaids. I get the boobs and the hair and all that, but they're like the ultimate tease. What about their fish bottom half? What are the sailors going to do with that?"

Sharon said, "That's a very hetero focus on male penetration you've got there, Miss Jenny."

Jenny looked confused.

"It's the singing," Maeve said, not looking up from her half-completed harbor scene. "They lure men onto the rocks with their beautiful voices."

THE RAIN STOPPED in the early evening. The sun blazed briefly before slowly sinking down, transforming the sky into the splendid sight you hope to see when you agree to a trip with people you're not sure you can tolerate for an entire week—washes of purples and pinks streaked with orange. Maeve started one team chopping vegetables in the kitchen and sent a second team to the deck to peel and devein five pounds of shrimp to go with grits: me, Sharon, Amy, Jenny, and another high school friend of theirs, Layla. Blond, toned Jenny resembled Amy in a way that left no doubt as to who was the copy and who was the original. Layla, on the other hand, wore gray and black, pulled off a cool shag haircut, and was the source of the cigarettes. She had a high-ranking corporate communications job she was very good at but didn't seem to like much. So far she'd mostly kept to herself, hanging out in the swinging bed or the hot tub with her iPad and her smokes. She was the only one there who'd never married.

We lined up our rockers facing the placid ocean and started peeling shrimp. We agreed it was a miracle nobody in the group had a shellfish allergy. A few families lingered on the sand. Kids swam and called to each other in the water. Sharon said she and Maeve had never been able to convince their son to swim in the ocean. He was afraid of the waves, the sharks, the jellyfish. Couples strolled, holding hands or throwing tennis balls for their eager dogs. I joked that the peeled shrimp looked like little flaccid gray penises, which got a decent laugh.

Everything was fine. Then Sharon said, "Let's all go around and tell . . ."

Sharon leads team-building retreats for nonprofits and—according to the website I made for her—she prizes her ability to guide difficult conversations in new directions. She's big on "Let's all go around and tell . . ."

Amy jumped in: ". . . the story of how we lost our virginity."

My hands stopped peeling. My brain threw its weight against the door that keeps the old, bad thing contained.

"Who can remember that far back?" Jenny said. More laughter.

"You go first," Sharon told Amy, "since it's your idea and your birthday."

Her boyfriend's car, when she was sixteen. They were totally in love and had no clue what they were doing.

"It was so awkward. But sweet."

Sharon did it with a girl at a camp that was supposed to cure her gayness.

Jenny did it in her parents' waterbed while they were out buying a new refrigerator.

A couple more women wandered out onto the porch with their wine and shared their stories.

"I think it was in a Mazda. It wasn't too roomy, and neither was I."

"I thought he'd never get it in, and then, when he finally did, it was over. It was like, oh, hello!...um, okay. Goodbye?"

They were all dying laughing. I tried to look like I was, too. It was Amy's birthday, and she was having fun—and she is not forgiving if you ruin a good vibe. When they got to me, I'd just lie. Not once had I told anyone about the bad thing that happened to me years ago, and I wasn't going to do it for the first time here. I'd learned my lesson about first times. Plus, several women on the trip photographed and posted every sandwich, sandcastle, baby with a hat (cute), baby without a hat (bad mommy), lost flip-flop, sunset, sunrise, etc. I had no desire to share my bad thing with these filterless people with no sense of privacy.

"He was my boss," one of them said.

"Whoa, hold up, your boss?"

"He was married, but he kept saying they were getting a divorce."

"Oh, one of those."

"I was so naive."

Everybody shook their heads in sympathy. The wind had stopped. The families on the beach packed up in the waning light. Far out in the Atlantic, a mass of pressure was working to become a storm worthy of a name.

Layla said, "My first time was when these two left me at a party and I got raped by a boy from our class."

All the rocking chairs on the porch went still.

"What?" Layla said, looking around at the rest of us. "I thought we were talking about this stuff now? Everything out in the open? Can't I me-too right now, if that's the answer to Sharon's question?"

Only Amy and Jenny didn't seem phased by what Layla had said. They'd clearly talked many times about what happened to Layla.

"We didn't *leave* you," Jenny said. "*You* wanted to stay."

Pretending to scratch, I discreetly felt my left breast, then the right. No lumps.

"I was drunk. You shouldn't have left me there."

Don't breathe. I didn't have to tell them anything. *Breathe.* I didn't have to listen either. All I had to do was stand up and go chop veggies with Maeve in the kitchen.

"We were drunk, too, Layla. And sixteen. We didn't know any better," Jenny said.

"I thought your *first* time was with Sean," Amy said.

Layla's story tumbled out, the three old friends moving the pieces around, arguing details. Afterward Amy had driven Layla to get an abortion. They hadn't told Jenny because she couldn't keep a secret. When Jenny found out about it later, her feelings were hurt.

The rest of us silently tore the spiny backs from the shrimp. These conversations are part of the Zeitgeist now. Or, as I'm calling it, the Shitegeist. Women the world over are telling their #MeToo stories—except for me. There's nobody's reaction I want to hear, and anyway, I'm fine, basically. Don't breathe. Breathe. I'm basically fine.

"Layla, your story sounds a lot like that whole thing with the woman and the Supreme Court guy," somebody said. "The party, I mean."

"That was, like, every party back then," Amy said.

"That thing she said about the laughter."

We all nodded, remembering it exactly, the yelling, braying laughter, the contests of boys.

"We thought you went off with that guy you liked," Jenny said to Layla.

"You didn't even *try* to find me. You just left." Layla's tone was matter of fact, no detectable tone of grievance. As though she'd chewed through her anger long ago and was done with it.

"Well, you were always bragging about making out with this guy, that guy," Jenny shrugged. "We just thought . . ."

Suddenly, there was only the sound of the waves and the rocking chairs. Everybody stopped peeling. Nobody said anything.

"What?" Jenny looked around. "*What?*"

Sharon stared at her. "What do you mean *what*? Why would you say that to her?"

"I'm just saying we all had guys do stuff to us—bad stuff—but we don't go blaming it on people who had nothing to do with it."

And then *Jenny* started to cry.

"Oh, good lord," Layla said. She went in the house and brought back a box of tissues.

Amy said, "Come on, Lay-lay, you know she didn't mean anything."

"She never does," Layla said, sitting back down in her rocker.

"Jenny, tell her you didn't mean anything."

Jenny dabbed her eyes and pouted.

"I didn't mean anything."

"You never do," Layla said, moving to the far end of the deck to light a cigarette.

"*Y'all!* It's my birthday," Amy scolded.

To my relief, the subject of first times and bad times was now closed. Within minutes, the three of them were on to a different old story, and the party seemed back on track. After dinner, several folks headed down to the beach. The cleanup team sang along to Alanis Morissette and Salt-N-Pepa as they did the dishes. Unsure which group to join, I drifted into the living room. The night-blackened wall of glass reflected the indoor scene: Sharon explaining to Jenny how to play Scattergories while Maeve handed out pencils and Amy poked her phone. I went up to the glass and cupped my hands over my eyes. Layla sat rocking on the deck by herself, drink in hand. I envied her solitude.

We played the game. Sharon perched on a blue ottoman near the windows. Now and then she peered out, making binoculars with her hands as I'd done. She reported what Layla was doing, just as she'd narrated the pelicans' behavior earlier that day.

Now they're hanging out on the end of the neighbors' pier. Now one's got a fish.

Now she's checking her phone. Now she's leaning on the railing. Now she's in the hot tub. I think she's naked.

"In the hot tub?" I said. "Is that safe? She's had a lot to drink."

"Don't worry about her," Jenny said. "That girl has a crazy high tolerance."

She and Amy laughed about all the times they'd seen Layla fucked up—too drunk to walk, too high to talk, too shit-faced to get to the toilet in time.

"Is that really funny still?" I asked.

"I guess not really..." said Amy.

"...But kind of," Jenny said, and they both fell to laughing again.

Then Amy said, "If she pukes in my hot tub, though, I'm going to be *pissed*."

I said I'd go check on her. Amy said I was an angel.

The ocean air felt refreshingly warm after the house's canned chill. Clothes littered the floor leading to the hot tub, which was sunk into a small deck projecting off the main deck, the tub an extravagant glowing circle of chemical blue. Layla's arms stretched along the rim, her head bowed toward the water. Her voice startled me.

"The fuck they have to sing about?"

Thank goodness she wasn't passed out. I doubted I was strong enough to haul her out of the water.

"Who?" I said.

She raised her head and looked up at me. Bubbles made a ruffle across the top of her breasts.

"The mermaids. What the fuck do they have to sing about? Combing their hair?"

Her own gray hair was slicked back, wet. The blue light made her face a little ghoulish.

"I just came to see if you're okay."

"Did Amy send you to see if I'm puking in her hot tub?"

"No, I *volunteered* to see if you were puking in her hot tub."

"Well, I'm not. Mainly because she would never let me forget it. She'd bring it up for the rest of my life, and I'd never live it down, and it would just go on the long list of stuff I do wrong, and I refuse to give her or Jenny the satisfaction."

"Okay."

"I'm not going to puke in her precious fucking hot tub, so come on in."

Joining her sounded much better than playing Scattergories. I stripped down to my underwear. The jetted water knocked me off-balance, and I felt clumsy as I flailed and caught at the side of the tub to steady myself.

"You okay?"

"I'm okay."

The water felt good. She commanded me to take off my bra, so I did.

"Better, right?"

"Yeah," I said, starting to relax. "This is nice."

"This. Is. Why. I. Came. On. This. Dumb. Trip." She smacked the water with each word. "To sit in the hot tub. And just fucking chill. With a naked stranger lady. Who I never met before. Who is a good fucking Samaritan. I came to just sit here and forget my life."

I laughed. "Me, too. I wanted to walk on the beach and sit in the hot tub and forget everything. And instead ..."

"You going to tell me your rape story, too?"

"Excuse me?"

Apparently, it had been happening all evening. Half the women there had cornered Layla, thinking they'd sniffed out a sympathetic ear.

"That's why I had to get so drunk, to *absorb* all that."

"I seriously just came to check on you."

"You can tell me if you want to. It's okay. People tell me their shit all the time. I have one of those faces. They think I'll understand how they feel, and I guess I kind of do, but a lot of the time, I also don't. Not really. I mean, all this time? I don't even understand how I feel about my *own* stuff."

This seemed like the one true thing that could be said. I nodded. We were quiet for a while, just listening to the tub and the ocean. Water, water, everywhere.

Then I said, "I know what they're singing about, the mermaids."

"What's that?"

"All the men they dragged down to the cold depths of the sea."

Layla's laugh broke open the night of tears. We stewed ourselves in Amy's beachside cauldron, and we laughed and laughed and, oh holy fuck, did we laugh.

WE WERE WHAT? Sixteen? Seventeen? Eighteen? All I remember is the beach game I agreed to play and the one I didn't. One minute a player, next minute a piece. The night like an iron pressing me into the damp sand. Grit embedded in my knees after they let me up.

Mine is not so different from Layla's story, not so different from a lot of stories, but it's part of me now. There's no procedure available to cut or burn or poison it out of me. No, forget that. I can't make a tumor metaphor out of it. I can't liken it to a hurricane, can't talk about it blowing over, or a quiet in the eye of the storm, or the deluge that follows the stillness.

I can't make a metaphor. I also can't give what happened to me a name because trying to name it is so fraught. As in: how big and how bad does a thing have to be to get a name? And what's the right name? Giving the thing a name—or calling what I say about it *a story*—would suggest that there's a way to make sense of it, and for me, my bad thing makes no sense. Never did, never will.

I said some version of this to Layla, or tried to. But I didn't attempt to tell exactly what happened.

"Telling it wouldn't change anything," I said. We were drinking even more, sweating together in the electric blue water. The moon raked a shine across the ocean.

"Have you ever told your daughters?"

"My girls are smarter than I was at their age."

"I wouldn't count on that." She put up her hands. "But I'm not a parent."

"Okay, but look," I said. "I'm going to say just this one more thing about it. Which is that my friends left me behind, just like Amy and Jenny left you."

"That sucks," Layla said.

"Yeah, thank you, but here's the thing. For the longest time I thought they *decided* to leave me there. But now, I'm pretty sure they *actually* just straight-up *forgot* me. I wasn't really part of their group, so they didn't think about me. It was just that I didn't matter to them at all, so they just forgot I was even there, and that's why they left me."

Under the water I felt my left breast. I didn't know if my heart was beating fast or it was just the tub vibrations. My younger child refused the left when nursing. Maybe she'd smelled something off about it.

"Do you think it's a myth?" Layla asked me. "About women and friendship? How good we are at it?"

"All I'm going to say is that after my friends left me behind that night, I learned to get a different sort of friends."

"And yet here you are," she said.

"Here *you* are."

"Here. We. Are."

WE STUMBLED IN after the others had gone to bed. I helped Layla get water and take Advil. We decided to sleep on the living room sofas so we wouldn't wake our respective roommates. I stationed a big plastic bowl on the pickled-wood floor next to her, settled her under a blanket, and patted her arm. I fell asleep instantly but woke up an hour later, parched. I shuffled to the kitchen and drank several glasses of water. The refrigerator hummed and the air-conditioning hummed and the waves shushed beyond the wall of glass.

Behind the house's many doors, women lay sleeping. Between the fourteen of us, we'd accumulated some seven hundred years of experience. Say we traveled back that amount of time, the year would be 1320, thereabouts. No Black Death yet, gunpowder just coming into use in the West. So many bad things yet to come down the pike.

In 1320, I imagined us like the medieval princesses pictured in stories I read as a child. Our crimson and emerald gowns belted with golden sashes, hippie-looking bands around our flowing hair. Some of us ventured nightly into the underworld and danced without fear until dawn, while others of us slumbered, waiting for princes.

Seven hundred years of life between us, and best I could tell, we'd not broken our enchantments yet.

I WAS THE ONE who ended up getting sick. I made it to the bathroom, but my retching woke up Amy. She swooped in to care for me, and now my flimsy tolerance has become the joke that won't die.

It's Day 5 now. Child Younger called this afternoon, asking for help with her math. Sure, I said, thinking it might be a relief to puzzle over something with a clear answer. But she texted me a photo of a page of word problems I was helpless to work out.

I said, "I'm sorry, honey. Maybe your sister can help you. She probably knows the formulas you're supposed to plug in."

I pictured them sitting together at the kitchen table, pencils scratching out runes.

"She's not talking to me. She's all mad at me over nothing."

She vented, listing all the ways her sister was unfair and mean. I'd been missing my daughters before she called, but listening to what I'd be dealing with when I got back, I dreaded going home. Home means facing whatever the doctor's going to say: cancer, not cancer (yet), or come back for more tests. Also, Layla thinks I should be honest with my girls about my bad thing, but I'm not sure. What will protect them more? Telling them a cautionary tale? Or keeping from them, for a bit longer, how shitty people can be?

I just want a little more time to not think about any of it.

"Look, it's only two more days. You'll just have to do the best you can. Try not to maim each other or burn down the house."

By 6:00 in the evening, it's cooler out. I head down to the beach by myself. It's low tide. People drift along the shoreline in pairs and trios. I trudge through the loose sand, then pick my way across the swath of sharp, broken shells to the firmer, darker sand where the walking is nicest.

Breathe, don't breathe, the tech said the other day, and I obeyed. I let her clamp my breast in a vise while my cheek mashed against that hulking machine. Radioactive waves zapped me as she stood protected behind her plexiglass shield, staring into her computer's blue light, scrolling and clicking. How obedient I was, so sure in that moment that I lived in a world designed to help me, not really comprehending how *that* was luxury.

I amble along the waterline, wetting my feet in the lapping tide. Ahead of me is a shirtless man relaxed in a folding chair. His eyes are closed; his sunburned hand holds a beer. Everything he needs is nearby: dirty white bucket, red cooler, blaring silver radio, crashing wine-dark sea. His fishing rod is anchored in a holder gouged into the sand. The thin line stretches out into the surf, invisible, but I know it's there because of how the rod bends toward the ocean. Not until I'm quite close does the sunlight catch the line so I can see it, a taut, shining filament stretching from the pole's tip to the water's undulating surface.

If the seated man forms a ninety-degree angle, and the rod is seven feet tall, and the fishing line forms the hypotenuse of a triangle whose longest side is the shifting sands beneath the man and the sea, where is the woman going, and what kind of fish is in danger of being caught?

To avoid the line, I have to change my path and take a wide arc around the man's back. I do this, then resume walking where I please. As I continue down the beach, I pray that a fish snatches the man's rod and tears away with it, making a beeline to the horizon. I conjure a real beast—taller than any man who has ever tried to vanquish it—riding the waves back to their source. A fish that's never been photographed, that can only be read about in stories. *The legends tell of a lip all stuck through with the hooks of men frenzied for the catch but never strong enough to haul it in.* A beat-looking old fish, nipped and chewed. Skin riddled with discolored patches, frayed fins, scales that refuse to glimmer.

No, not a fish after all: a leviathan whose soundings reverberate like low and eerie laughter—laughter that echoes in men's ears as they're forced to cut bait before their lines snap and send them reeling.

The light is fading, but I keep going forward, same as I did when I walked—no phone or wallet or water—along that hot road leading from the boys who used me to the girls who left me behind. Now I choose to walk. But back then I sorely wished I didn't have to trudge along, hungover under a dawn sun already scorching. That I could keep going—with my feet blistering and my mouth sour—confused me. Before that night, I'd thought if a truly bad thing happened to you, you must immediately fall over dead. I couldn't imagine how people lived after suffering.

I've never seen a sunrise since and not thought of that hot sun. That morning, I was sure not another soul could ever know how lost I was. Seldom since have I been more baffled as to how I've come to a particular moment. I honestly didn't know what I'd done to get there. And yet I blamed myself, as though I'd hooked my own lip and said, *Pull, everybody. Pull.*

At the Arrowhead

Sharla has been taking money from Mr. Nichols in Room 423. While he's in the bathroom, she slips a five or ten out of his cracked leather wallet and stuffs it in her pocket. She looks through the window at the geyser in the middle of the green man-made lake and waits for him to call out, *Hey girl.* The woman who used to have this room called her *honey.* The one before that, *sugar.* Mr. Nichols doesn't want her in the bathroom with him the whole time, like some residents do, but he needs help transferring from toilet to wheelchair, wheelchair to bed. In January, he could still do it by himself. Now it's July.

"Hey! Hey, girl!"

After cleaning up Mr. Nichols, she gets him back into his wheelchair. She might be closing in on fifty, or maybe it's closing in on her, but she's strong. Ten years she's been doing this job, and before that she did other hard work, on her feet all day, moving and lifting and smiling, in restaurants, stores, a nursery school. She's always told potential employers that she doesn't mind working hard because she's the kind of person who likes to keep busy. It's what she tells Nurse Jill, who tries to load her up with work beyond what she thinks Sharla can handle. What Nurse Jill doesn't know is, she is only one of many who have tried to break Sharla.

Parked before the playing television with his soft drink, Mr. Nichols says, as he always does, *Thank you.* She says, *You're welcome.* Good manners are something nobody can take away from you, her grandmother used to say. It doesn't hurt anybody to be civil. Sharla taught her children the same.

Not all the residents are civil to Sharla. They have groped her. They have called her ugly things because they look at her hair and think she is mixed. Maybe she is—how would she know—but her mother had the same hair, and she was white. Some residents talk to Sharla like she's stupid, others like she's a person they knew long ago, a person they loved, or didn't. A few don't talk at all. She doesn't hold any of this against them. They can't help what they do. They are old, lonely, sick people: confused, many of them, and all of them tired.

Together, Sharla and Mr. Nichols watch history unspooling on the television, the day's new horrors and absurdities recalling moments from other decades, as far back as the 1940s for Mr. Nichols, for Sharla mostly the seventies and eighties. Everything's happening again, he says, and she asks if he thinks it's worse this time, the way people are saying. He's not sure, but they agree it's a shame—the world, the way people do today.

In a minute, she'll leave his room to go help somebody else. She won't take anything from that resident, nor the next one, nor the next: each of them sitting in their separate rooms—close, but apart, like eggs in a carton. She only takes from Mr. Nichols. What he did was a long time ago, but she can't forget it.

AT HOME SHE changes the sheets and cleans the bathroom. Her stepdaughter Crystal is coming from Winston-Salem to stay the weekend. Sharla doesn't like living alone. When her Donnie left, her last child to go off to college, she woke at 2:00 a.m. every night for weeks, convinced she was having a heart attack. Her children are everything to her. She ended it with her first two husbands because they just could not be decent to the children. If Rusty wasn't ignoring them, he was scaring them to death, and Al just picked, picked, picked: nobody could do a damn thing right.

Her third husband, Chase, was sweet with the kids, but you couldn't really count on him for anything but trouble. "Ha, ha, you should've known he was a cheater from his name," said a girl she used to work with, thinking it was okay to make fun because Sharla must be hardened to her marriages breaking up. "You know, because he chases tail," the girl said, assuming after Sharla didn't laugh that she didn't get the joke.

As usual, Sharla was too busy at work to eat lunch, so she heats up a can of Italian wedding soup. It's surprising she can tolerate canned soup, given how much of it she ate growing up, but it still feels like a luxury that she can afford now not to stretch it with water. She eats quickly, washes her dishes, then walks Jamie, her brown-and-white rat terrier—what a face that dog has, as knowing as a person—and while he's sniffing and peeing, she tries to call Donnie. He doesn't answer. No surprise. She hopes it means that he still has work and maybe isn't drinking too much or doing other stuff she'd rather he didn't. Maybe today some boy isn't actively breaking Donnie's heart. When you get down to it, that might be all a person can hope for on any given day.

She could call Donnie's sister, but Jean is not the person to talk to if you're low. In the last few years, Jean has taken to a stern form of religion befitting her natural lack of humor. Since the election—that long night when Sharla poured champagne down the sink and cried, wishing, among many other things, that her son had a different nickname—Jean and Donnie have stopped talking altogether. Each of them thinks the other is going to Hell, which distresses Sharla. It also distresses her that Jean and her husband won't allow their two children, Sharla's only grandbabies, to watch cartoons, go trick-or-treating, or read books with any kind of magic in them. She has never been allowed to keep them overnight.

Maybe she doomed Jean to being an unhappy person by displaying her own misery too openly when the kids were small. Once, during the bad spell when she and Rusty were fighting constantly because they were almost over, Sharla put peanut butter sandwiches and glasses of milk on the coffee table and told Crystal she was going out to get gas. Sharla was twenty-two, and Jean had just turned three, and Crystal was almost eleven. The girls were watching *Looney Tunes*, and Rusty was God knows where, and jealous, neglected Sharla was losing her damn mind. An hour down the highway, she turned around, and it shames her always to remember how she thought she was coming back for Rusty—not Crystal, not Jean.

When Crystal shows up, she wants to go out dancing and get as drunk as possible. That's the last thing Sharla feels like doing, but she agrees because Crystal's husband has accused her of having known before they married that she was unable to bear children.

"I never thought he was the cruel type," Sharla says, putting on mascara at her wonderful old makeup mirror with the lights up the sides. Her girls used to fight to sit in front of it and pretend they were movie stars.

"They're all cruel," Crystal says, her voice muffled. She's in the closet, trying to find an outfit Sharla can wear dancing. She pulls out the dress bought with Mr. Nichol's fives and tens. It's the color of the garnet ring Sharla's grandmother used to let her hold to the light so she might see the stones turn from dull, blackish chips to flashing red jewels.

"This is pretty," Crystal says. "I like the neckline. But it's not a dress for dancing."

"No," Sharla agrees. "It's not."

The next morning, Crystal's hangover doesn't stop her from suiting up. "Come on," she says to Sharla. "It's so hot. A swim would do you good."

The water in her apartment complex pool is alluring, so blue and cool looking, but Sharla must go in to work. Mr. Nichols is in bed, face to the wall, his back turned on the photographs his daughters have arranged around the small room—color pictures of children in dance costumes and sports uniforms, a portrait of his dead wife, black-and-white photos of earlier generations. The one Sharla has studied most is a 1970s family portrait from Sears: the wife with an outdated (even then) bubble of brown hair; a toothy girl in a flowered dress and red yarn hairbows; a smaller girl dressed the same; a baby in the wife's lap, the boy, soon to be as irrevocably spoiled as Sharla's Donnie; and him, of course, Mr. Nichols. Not bad looking if you can get past the fashion of the day—big tinted glasses, sideburns, sandy turtleneck. It's exactly how he looked when he used to stay at the Arrowhead, the first place Sharla remembers living with her mother and brother.

Up Highway 29 toward Virginia, the Arrowhead had been a long brick building lined with doors. Out front beside the road, the motel's name unfurled across a giant 1950s turquoise sign shaped, of course, like an arrowhead. That sign in its heyday had been the shit, but by Sharla's time, it was just shitty. The lights running round it had burned out, the flamboyant script faded nearly away, and a brown crack was spreading, year by year, right down the middle. Every day when Sharla got off the school bus in the parking lot, kids patted their hands against their mouths and dumbly war cried. *Woo-woo-woo-woo.*

While Sharla gets Mr. Nichols's clothes ready, she talks cheerfully, hoping to rally him. She asks what he did for work when he was younger.

"I was in sales. On the road a lot. I lived half my life in motels."

Me, too, she doesn't say.

Finally, he agrees to get up and sit in the wheelchair. His tray has come, and she opens his milk and unwraps his straw. Head cocked like a curious bird, he watches her actions as though he might learn to do them one day.

A few minutes later, struggling to get his eggs on the fork and lift them to his mouth, he says thoughtfully, "You find out quick how little you need when you're never at home."

Breakfast over, she gives him a chance to get out of his pajama shirt without her help, but his fingers are too stiff to work the buttons today. When she bends forward to help, he grabs her hair. She freezes, stifles a protest, waits.

His hand falls back to his lap. He only wanted to touch it.

"I know you," he says.

"That's right. I'm Sharla. I'm here to help you get dressed."

"No, no." He tilts his head again, thinking, trying to recognize her more fully. "I know you from before."

People used to remark how much Sharla looked like her mother, which made her feel two ways—proud, because her mother had been pretty, and also angry, because the only time she'd ever wanted to resemble her mother was when she was trying to irritate her grandmother.

"Where do you know me from, Mr. Nichols?" she asks, wondering what she will say if he can put it all together.

Concentrating on her face doesn't help him place her. He shakes his head.

"I know you. I know you, Sharla."

HER MOTHER, WHO made the children call her Becky, had been the housekeeper at the Arrowhead, and as a special favor, the manager allowed the three of them to live on the back side in Room 28, the end room with the stained carpet and dribbly shower. Its window looked out on a strip of pavement and a thick piney wood. Even though she didn't much like the way the manager talked to Becky when his wife wasn't around, Sharla tried to be polite because he allowed her and Donovan to play in the pool whenever they wanted. Her earliest memory is of pulling Donovan around the shallow end in a purple inflatable ring sporting the head of Dino, the pet from the Flintstones. Sharla would set Donovan inside the ring, he'd put his arms around Dino's neck, and off they'd go, Sharla towing him through the water. Donovan was her very own baby, and the pool was hers, too, the motel her private mansion, and all the cars parked in the lot her personal property—the nice ones anyway.

The guests were mostly men on business and families breaking up long drives to nicer locales—beach houses or grandmas' houses or cities with real sights to see. She tended to get along well with the kids passing through, but Donovan always splashed too hard or took their snacks without asking. He freaked them out, cussing or faking a convulsion, so they'd swim off to the deep end, inviting only Sharla to join them. Always he would cry to Becky, who claimed that it broke her heart to think she'd raised a girl cruel enough to exclude her own brother.

When Sharla was seven, Becky started giving her a dollar a week to help vacuum the rooms. Motel guests, usually men, gave Sharla fifty cents or a dollar because she was "real cute" or "real smart," but she knew it was really because she was poor. She put up with their condescension because she liked having money in her pocket. Her favorite thing was to go next door to the diner and treat herself to a hamburger and a slice of key lime pie. Though often full of people and noise, the bright, clean diner was a place where Sharla felt calm. Nobody minded if she leaned her forehead against the cool glass of the dessert case so she could marvel at the high peaks of meringue, the dizzying swirls of frosting, the rich, tempting colors—chocolate brown, lemon yellow, berry red, sugar white. The waitresses took their smoke breaks at her booth, chatting about boyfriends and clothes and trips to Holden Beach or Grandfather Mountain. Sharla was happy to listen to them, but she preferred having the booth all to herself, the solitude a luxury: no Donovan to watch, no Becky to please or avoid. Napkin in her lap, slurping leisurely at her Coke, Sharla would choose houses from the real estate magazines off the wire rack by the bubblegum machine. She'd gaze around the restaurant and select a man for Becky. Occasionally, she'd pick one out for herself.

One day, after such a lunch, she went back to 28 and turned her key in the lock, only to find the chain on. The door opened just enough for her to see that the room was dark, the curtains drawn. Shape-shifting on the bed was one figure, then two, then one again. On the carpet lay her mother's sky-blue panties, a man's shoes.

She ran to the pool, where Donovan was paddling around on a raft in the deep end.

"Get down to the three-foot, dummy! You can't touch there!" she yelled.

Donovan stuck out his tongue and relaxed on his raft as though taking a sunbath. Sharla kicked off her shoes and dove in. She swam to the raft, flipped it, and dragged her brother, sputtering and fighting, to the shallow end. Out of the pool, she spanked him hard, a thing their mother had told her she must never do to her little brother. He didn't tell on her, but he didn't forget it either. That night, Becky, suddenly flush with cash, took them to the diner for a treat. It was too much for Sharla to eat there twice in one day, and it made her sick.

HOME FROM HER SHIFT, she fixes a dinner of popcorn and ice cream to enjoy with Crystal in front of the TV like they used to when Crystal was little and Sharla and Rusty were still in love. The romantic comedy they watch makes them weepy, and they laugh at themselves for being so silly. Sharla doesn't want Crystal to leave the next day. She thinks of asking her to come live with her if she can't work things out with her husband, but she decides it's too soon. Also, she's afraid of what she'll feel if Crystal says no.

They brush their teeth and get into bed; the dog snuggles between their legs. Crystal admits that one reason she's sad not to have children of her own is that she has always wanted to show Sharla what a good mom she could be.

"I wanted to be like you," she says, her voice in the dark timid, the way it sounded when Sharla first met her. "So you'd be proud of me."

"Oh, baby," Sharla says, hugging Crystal close. "Who wouldn't be proud of you?"

They aren't just words. Crystal used to cry because she wished Sharla was her real mom. Sharla would hug her tight and say, "You're not my blood, baby, but you're my heart." That wasn't just words either.

You're my heart was what Sharla's mother used to say to them before she headed out into the night. Once Donovan was asleep, Sharla would cut off the TV and watch the white numbers of the clock radio flip. If she got too scared pondering what might be lurking in the woods behind the motel, she'd turn the music on. In the mornings, she'd wake to find her mother always there, sprawled in the other double bed, dark curls rampant on the pillow.

Not until Rusty left her did Sharla realize how lonely her mother must have been, raising two children alone in a seedy motel. How many times had Sharla's grandmother Constance said to teenage Sharla, running wild, that she was going to wind up just like her mother, who, at seventeen, had refused Constance's offer to pay for an abortion (illegal then) and to never tell Becky's father—drugstore owner, Presbyterian deacon, Rotarian. Becky's hippie shenanigans had already given him one heart attack, and Constance hoped to avert another. The poor man had not worked so hard to bring himself up out of the mill village for shame to be his reward. He disowned Becky and later did the same to Sharla when she left college at UNC Greensboro to have Rusty's baby. By the time Rusty ran off, her grandfather was dead, and her grandmother, tired of losing the people she loved, let Sharla and Jean move in with her. Then Sharla met Al and left Constance again.

MR. NICHOLS'S DAUGHTERS no longer resemble their photographs. The one who's about Sharla's age is gray coiffed and heavily made up. This Sunday, she wears a kaftan of embroidered teal linen. She rears back in Mr. Nichols's recliner to elevate her swollen ankles, while her bony older sister moves nervously around the room, straightening things that don't need it, checking for signs that her father is being improperly cared for. Again, Mr. Nichols has stayed in bed and is facing the wall.

"Why is he like this? He wasn't like this last time. Is he on new meds?" the skinny one barks at Sharla.

"She doesn't know. She's just the aide," says the other, scrolling through her phone, diamonds winking desperately on her plump fingers.

When they've gone and Sharla is waiting for Mr. Nichols to finish in the bathroom, she opens his bureau drawer and sees that his billfold is not in its usual place. Her breath clutches. What if they've figured out that she's been taking his money? She doesn't want to get fired. She likes it here. Her children say she's too smart to spend her days wiping old people's butts. They don't understand why she likes caring for people who need her so much. Of course, there are things she wouldn't miss: staff meetings, performance reviews, all the regulations made up by people who never tried to do her job. But she loves talking with Holly at the front desk, Clarence and Tank in the kitchen, Ernesto the maintenance man, Nurse Allison, and her fellow aides—Rainbow, Kim, LaNiece, and Mary. She would miss the holiday parties and the occasional nights out for coworkers' birthdays. If she had to leave, she'd miss the Griffins in 307, still fighting after sixty years of marriage; Mrs. Trilling, still reading *Popular Mechanics* at 98; and Mr. Jenkins, still sporting a tie every day to impress the ladies.

"Hey, girl!"

She cleans him up and helps him change into fresh pajamas. Seeing how the effort tires him, she lets him rest as much as he needs to between each task. On the television, dark-suited men anxiously watch as the president talks. Later, in the staff room, Rainbow will ask, *Did y'all hear the Cheeto showing his ass again?* Kim will say that she, for one, appreciates a politician who isn't afraid to do what needs to be done to keep real Americans safe. Sharla, as always, will say nothing and not be sure if that is right.

Once Mr. Nichols is in bed and all set for the night, Sharla stacks his dishes to go back to the kitchen.

"Hey," he says, softer this time. He's holding out the billfold.

"Can you put this back in my drawer?" His voice is raspy from disuse. "I have to hide it from them. All they want with me is my money."

IN THE SUMMER of 1977, Sharla was nine, Donovan was five, and Mr. Nichols had to have been a little past forty. One afternoon, while she was floating in the pool, and her brother was coloring at the umbrella table, Mr. Nichols asked Donovan what he was drawing. Lying on one of the orange loungers, his hairy belly soft above the waistband of his swim trunks, he was drinking beer from a can.

"You drawing a dog, buddy? Or a cat? I like cats."

Donovan ignored him. Mr. Nichols, smiling, tried to catch Sharla's eye, but she turned her head. She wasn't there to be his friend.

"A house? A car?"

Donovan shook his head, the look on his face not merely serious but affronted. When Sharla saw Jean wearing the exact same expression years later, her heart almost stopped.

"Plane? Robot?"

The boy shook his head harder and harder with each question—fire truck? monster?—until it began to look like he was having a seizure.

"Is it a shark? Maybe a lion?"

Donovan convulsed a final time, then shot out of the chair and ran toward Mr. Nichols, fists pummeling the air, shouting, "A rocket! Okay? It's a goddamn rocket!"

He stood over Mr. Nichols, fists raised, ready to smash right down into the white dough of his belly. *Do it*, Sharla thought. She was hanging on the pool's edge now, watching.

But Mr. Nichols wasn't alarmed. He sipped his beer and said, "Well, buddy, can I see it? I think rockets are neat."

And to Sharla's amazement, Donovan, who never willingly did one thing anybody asked him to do, got the drawing and carried it over to show Mr. Nichols.

For weeks, Mr. Nichols brought Donovan little gifts when he came to stay: a t-shirt, a coin sorter, a remote-control car. Sharla, he looked right through. And Becky? Although she always greeted him the same as she did any other customer—politely, remotely—on the nights he stayed at the motel, Becky always went out. Sharla knew it wasn't a coincidence. Nor did she think it a coincidence when her mother began talking happily about how they might soon get an apartment, where Sharla and Donovan would have their own room with a bunk bed, and she'd teach Sharla to cook on a real stove instead of a hot plate.

All summer, Donovan worked frantically on his rockets, coloring them red and green, or orange and purple, each one shooting off into a dark blue space full of ringed planets; pocked moons; jagged, many-cornered stars; and a yellow sun so big it threatened to burn everything else right off the page. As for Sharla, she was tan and full of muscle, swimming for nothing but the joy of it.

On July 27, she took herself to the diner. She was already beginning to dread going back to school, but maybe, if Becky was telling the truth, they'd be in an apartment by then, and she'd never again have to endure the humiliation of being woo-wooed off the bus. Forty years later, Sharla still remembers that lunch with exceptional clarity—how she licked her finger, poked up the French fry salt from her plate, and licked her finger again. She remembers how good the salt tasted, the last crisp sips of Coke. Digging into her terrycloth pockets, she found the quarters she had ready for a tip and laid them on the table: one, two. It felt good being in a position to be generous.

As she crossed the parking lot, she could smell the blacktop softening under the sun's power. In the pool, Donovan's red raft was floating in the deep end. No doubt he'd gone inside, into the air conditioning, to watch the *Young and the Restless* with the manager's wife. Sharla had her swimsuit on under her clothes, the way she always did that summer. She took off her shorts and t-shirt and headed for the ladder at the shallow end. She knew better than to dive right after a meal. She would simply ease in and retrieve the raft so the manager wouldn't fuss about Donovan leaving it there; then she'd wait her thirty minutes before swimming.

It wasn't until she'd slid into the water and started to tow the raft that she saw Donovan half under it, face down and too still. She grabbed him and swam one-armed toward the ladder, strong with panic. Out on the hot concrete, she rolled him onto his stomach and watched the water run out of his mouth, then rolled him onto his back and tried to breathe life between his cold blue lips, as she'd seen done on television. Behind her, the cars and trucks whipped up and down Highway 29. The noise of their constant, oblivious rushing had long been so familiar that she'd stopped hearing it. But that afternoon it suddenly registered, louder than ever, the sound of all the world passing her by without stopping to help.

Her mother had screamed when she heard that Sharla hadn't watched Donovan and kept him safe. She'd fallen to the floor, cried a while, then lurched up to strike Sharla, who had not tried to run but simply, out of instinct, raised her arms to shield her face. Her mother's blame seemed the only fitting response to what had happened. Accepting the blows, she feared Becky might kill her and half wished she would. But the manager intervened, and a week later, Sharla sat by herself in front of the TV in Room 28 all afternoon, then all evening, then all the next day, until, finally, the manager's wife knocked and said, "Your grandmother's come for you, Sharla." Then a voice, a woman's voice she'd never heard before, said, "The child's name is Charlotte." And after that, for as long as she and her grandmother lived together, it was.

THE CEMETERY WHERE her grandparents and Donovan are buried is a big place, acres of grass and gray stones, few trees, an abundance of sky. Sunday afternoon, following her shift, Sharla and Crystal go there to meet Jean. Sharla is wearing the garnet dress and a new pair of heels. In the end, the money she took from Mr. Nichols was a little short—she had to kick in seven dollars—but these are the nicest shoes she's ever had, the leather as soft as young skin, alive and supple. Crystal looks professional in her bank teller's gray blazer and skirt; Jean wears an oddly girlish light blue dress with a drop waist and a wide, white collar.

"I see Mr. All About Me couldn't join us today," Jean says, Bible in hand.

"Your brother had to work," Sharla lies. She spoke to Donnie earlier; he was apologetic but adamant that he could not see Jean so long as she belonged to a gay-bashing cult. And although Sharla would've liked all her children to be there to put flowers on their uncle's grave on the fortieth anniversary of his death, she didn't fuss because she couldn't bear to hear Jean telling Donnie for the umpteenth time that God loves the sinner but not the sin, and Donnie telling Jean to go fuck herself.

The bouquet Crystal picked up is only from the grocery store and doesn't have a fragrance, but it's real. Constance would never have put trashy plastic flowers on Donovan's grave; she brought only fresh arrangements, which Sharla had to hold in the car, blooms tickling her nose and water sloshing onto her legs and soaking through her pantyhose no matter how carefully her grandmother drove.

"Do you want me to say a prayer?" Jean asks.

"All right." Sharla has always tried to let her children do what they're good at, even when what they're good at is not something she can really get behind.

Though Sharla bows her head and closes her eyes, she barely listens. When they lost Donovan, it wasn't the first time she'd encountered death. Once at the Arrowhead, a man had shot another man in the parking lot. Her mother had warned her and Donovan away from the window as they listened to the escalating argument, the two pops of the gun, the car speeding away, the sirens. It had sounded just like the television programs they weren't supposed to watch but heard all the time through the thin walls—only this time much louder, the excitement immediate and thrilling.

At the Arrowhead, once, a woman staying alone in Room 14 swallowed dozens of pills and lay down with a *Glamour* magazine. When Becky found her, there was a cigarette butt in her curled hand, smoked down to the filter. Whenever Sharla went to vacuum 14 afterward, she wondered at that woman casually turning pages and smoking, as though waiting for death was no different than waiting for anything else.

The day after Donovan died, Mr. Nichols came around, smoking a cigarette and carrying a boy's navy pinstripe suit, a white shirt, a necktie with a rocket on it, and a brand-new pair of shoes—all of it to be wasted underground, and nothing for her. Now, forty years later, wearing the dress and shoes his money paid for, she feels as though she has dressed for her own funeral rather than the one she wasn't allowed to go to. Hearing Jean say the prideful, accusatory words the poor girl mistakes for prayer, Sharla thinks that she ought to have insisted that Donnie come today and stand next to his sisters, even if he can't talk to Jean, and Jean can't talk to him. She thinks she will put all of Mr. Nichols's money back. Maybe she'll stand too long with the cash in her hand, and Nurse Jill will catch her and get her fired. Maybe she won't put the money back. It doesn't matter. The money's not important.

One day soon, Sharla knows, she'll go in to wake Mr. Nichols, but he will be done with his waking. Outside, the shining relentless geyser will continue shooting up, the beads of water raining back down to make the perpetual white circle that is always on the surface of the lake. Sharla will hold the old man's hand for a few minutes. That's what she always does for her residents who can no longer wake up, because she would want it done for her. She'll try not to think long about how he put that same hand on her mother's skin. Instead, she will try, is trying now, to think of how gently, how lightly, how kindly, Mr. Nichols touched her brother's shoulder as he showed his drawings. She wishes she could think only of that but finds herself powerless to keep out the memory she least wants, the one she would like to lose forever: Donovan face down, his new trunks ballooning, their buoyancy useless as she, sitting oblivious in the diner, tastes salt, and dreams. Nor can she stop remembering Mr. Nichols, yesterday, touching her hair and saying, "I know you," and how she didn't say, *Yes, yes, you do.*

Cleopatra's Needle

Fuck one middle-aged man and next thing you know you're in New York City, hottest summer on record, hotter than the goddamn Summer of Sam, working for some stupid company—Gimp & Gimpel, Lamestein and Lamerstein, I can't even remember the name.

The irony is that I don't even like middle-aged men because they are always trying to tell you what to do. We only did it a few times, twenty-five, maybe thirty, I can't really remember because usually we were drunk. Not just tipsy—I mean existentialist despair drunk, face the firing squad without a shred of hope drunk, utterly dead drunk. What can I say? We felt we had a lot to be sad about, I guess. At least he did, and then I caught it like the chicken pox.

The whole problem with this middle-aged man is that he is the estranged husband of my mother's dearest friend, and I know it sounds tacky, but it's a very complex situation.

At work I feel too lonely and helpless to sit at my desk for more than five minutes. I go to the bathroom, get coffee, talk to the mail girl, make unnecessary copies—anything to look busy and stay sane.

Bernard, who shares my cubicle, says, "If you don't watch out, Pauline's going to bitch at you for being away from your desk too much."

"Thanks for the warning," I say.

"I'm just saying. I've gotten in trouble for that myself."

"I'm always in trouble anyway," I say, "so it doesn't bother me."

I'm telling the truth. Apparently I have always been a "trouble-maker." I am twenty-four now, and this is still true. My mother called me this very thing the last time I was home, but it didn't sound as funny as it did when I was in high school.

The things I used to get in trouble for were so stupid. For instance, in tenth grade, I told Coach Atkins I couldn't do gym because I was a hermaphrodite and all that jumping might cause my testicles to finally descend, and I would be really embarrassed if a testicular sac was suddenly flopping around in my gym shorts. Now, I thought that was funny, and if Coach wanted to be so literal-minded, it's not my fault.

A few times I dropped lit cigarettes into some trash cans on the school grounds and set fire to them. When they sent me to the guidance counselor, I couldn't say for sure whether or not I meant to do it—I didn't think so. I mean, I was a teenager. I was thinking of more important things. When will I get laid? Will everybody on earth be wiped out by some uber-virus before I fulfill my dream of making a Joan of Arc suit out of bottle caps and picture wire? Will we get wiped out before I get laid?

Bernard says to me, "You know you're putting those forms in the wrong basket. The finished ones are supposed to go over here."

He has nice hair, pretty eyes. I like his shoes. But he is pissing me off. "Thank you, Bernard."

Am I in love with Mr. Middle-Aged Man? I don't think so, but I think about him an awful lot. Honestly, the whole thing is very painful.

Bernard says, "Uh, Leckie, you're in the wrong screen, that's why you can't put in that order."

Bernard has a picture of his cat up over his computer. I think this is highly endearing. I say, "Why don't you mind your own business, dickweed."

"Hey, I'm just trying to help," says Bernard. He has that facial expression of *whoa, what a bitch*. "If you want to get fired that's your problem."

"Okay. If you want me to kick you in your fucking teeth, that's your problem. So just keep talking to me and you'll see." I start typing, figuring there's no more to be said, but now Bernard is talking to himself. His monologue is abusive—I hear words like *bitch* and *crazy* and *loser*.

I swivel my chair to look at him. He's bent over his desk, writing on some form, a CR-290 or a PO or up-yours 2000. I can't keep all these fucking forms straight. The human race was not created to fill out forms—we're in the midst of devolution, but that's another subject. Bernard is so cute. It just breaks my heart to hear those filthy words rush out of his sweet, clean mouth. Before I can do anything about it, I'm crying myself into a frenzy.

I put my head on a stack of forms and let my torrent of snot and tears and slobber ruin them.

Even when Bernard begins to apologize and pat my back, I can't stop. I try to tell myself it's not normal to weep this way at work. I hiccup and cough and try to stop, but the more I try to stop, the more I cry. Ultimately I hyperventilate and somebody hands me a little paper sack to breathe into. Every time I breathe, I suck up somebody's muffin crumbs. The bag crackles as it fills and empties, and gradually I get interested in the soothing regularity, the way the bag resembles a bellows or a lung. I wonder if I'm transferring muffin crumbs from this little paper lung into my own real lung.

When I open my eyes, feeling deflated and curiously affectionate toward the little paper sack, there's a crowd of interested faces above my cubicle panel.

Pauline takes me into her office and gives me a bottle of water. She asks me if I'm going to cry anymore. I tell her no, ma'am, and she tells me to save that for my grandmother. Pauline seems very New York—she's got that whole "ugly glasses make me look smart" thing going on. Her hair looks like she sleeps on razor blades. Her suit looks like crushed money.

She lectures me about how I'm late every day, and away from my desk too often, and how I make too many mistakes in my data entry, and also they still can't find that file I "misplaced" two weeks ago, which may or not be the file I mailed to a fake address because I didn't feel like dealing with it.

"I'm really sorry," I say.

"And sleeping. Do you know I've seen you sleeping at your desk on three separate occasions?" She puts her head way back—she looks like she's trying to look *under* her glasses at me.

"I like to take a nap during lunch break."

Blah, blah, blah about how my lunch break doesn't start at 9:00 a.m.

Pauline has a very nervous nature. She messes with her hair a lot while she's talking. She performs so many fidgety tricks with her ballpoint pen that I want to ask if she ever twirled baton. Finally, she suggests that I'm very upset and distracted by something, and maybe I should tell her what it is so she can recommend a therapist. These New Yorkers crack me up. You can't find lightbulbs in the grocery store, they want to send you to therapy. I cried already—what do I need therapy for?

But I hate to disappoint her. I stare at her. I let my eyes go wide like a scared animal. My lower lip trembles. I squeeze out a little wash of tears. All very natural.

I say, "It's my brother. He's very ill. He's only two years older than me—we're so close, we're almost like twins. He's crazy about me. I didn't want to leave him, but he said, no, Leckie, it's your dream to go to New York, you should go. And he is such an amazing person. He was going to be an animator. He did this cartoon—you'd just love it. It's about Joan of Arc—every week the voices tell her to do different things."

I'm getting that adrenaline rush, and she's eating it up. She loves it that my brother is going to die any day, that I don't have enough money to go home to see him, that I had a locket with his picture in it and just this very morning the chain broke and it got lost down a grate.

Afterwards we go out together to get coffee and smoke. Pauline says she feels like a jerk for being mean to me. She says she's going to talk to the benefits officer and see if they can't get me some time off even though it's still my probation period. She can't hear enough about Peter, my brother. What a nice name he has, a saint's name.

TO BE FAIR, you should know how the whole thing with Mr. Middle-Aged Man started. Because I think you think I am just some slut home-wrecker, and that's not how it was. First, he was already separated and had been for a while. Second, I have loved him and his whole family my entire life. Our families used to go to the beach together. His kids used to stay at our house when he and his wife went out of town. I'm crazy about every person in his family.

Picture a wedding in the country, on the coast, in the yard of a ramshackle old house with peeling white paint and a tin roof. Women in thin flowered dresses and hats, men ruddy with sun and drink, garlands of flowers swagging from tree to tree like jungle vines. Picture me there, drinking champagne and dancing to the band with a lady singer. There's about four hundred other people doing the same thing. Among them are my parents, their friends whose marriage is breaking up, and the children of those friends. The smell of smoking pig is in the air.

In the dark blue sky over the marsh hangs a ripe white moon. A breeze brushes the tall grass and ripples the water, disperses the barbecue smoke and carries the voice of the lady singer into the pine trees on the other side of the house. I'm standing among the parked cars sneaking a smoke because even though I have been out of college for two years, I still don't smoke in front of my parents. The crickets and frogs are screaming.

He's looking for me. I see him thread his way between the cars. He's had a little to drink, not too much. I've had a little myself.

He asks if I'd like to take a walk. He is sad that his life is ruined, and I'm sad for him and the way everything has turned out. I say

yeah, let's take a walk. He offers his hand, and we walk away from
the drunk people, the flickering flames of tiki torches, the ropes of
flowers hanging tree to tree, the decimated pig, the rambling white
house, the scramble of cars on the lawn. We walk down the sandy
alley that leads back to the road. We go away, into the woods just a
little. He takes me by the hand into the tall, rough pines, away from
the lapping marsh and its waving grasses, back into the trees where
it is quiet but for the distant song of the lady singer and where the
moonlight is filtered and the ground is matted with thin, damp nee-
dles. Down he pulls me into the soft, forgiving dirt, down I go and pull
him over me, down I pull him and down he presses and up, up, I look
into the tall, rough pines.

He spoke to me. I won't tell you what he said. Just that he made me
beautiful to myself. Can you blame me?

HE IS SUPPOSED to be in town tomorrow, Saturday, on some kind
of business. He said his schedule is very full, but if he can, he will
meet me in the roof garden on top of the Metropolitan Museum of
Art. I think it's hokey, but I say okay, whatever. Now that I know him
better, I realize he has a very Mr. Middle-Aged Man approach to romance. But I'm lonely, so I say okay. I'll meet you tomorrow, Saturday, the day after I've told the people at work that I have a dying
sweet brother named Peter who once received a letter from the Dalai
Lama. Peter, who taught a troubled boy to tap-dance.

Saturday I am happy first thing because there is some kind of eth-
nic parade on television. It's in Queens. These New Yorkers are the
damnedest for giving parades. There's all the time somebody hav-

ing a parade—Irish, Dominicans, Greeks, veterans, queers, Thanksgiving, antifur, whatever. I just love it. It puts me in my best can-do spirit.

I get dressed in my black pique cigarette pants and crimson spaghetti strap tank top. Leckie, my mother would say if she could see me now, you look like a hooker. Why can't you wear something more sophisticated? It's 1995! You're living in the age of feminism, Leckie, do something about it! You don't have to get dolled up and display yourself like a piece of meat. When I was your age, I rebelled by living with a guitar player in Myrtle Beach. But you don't have to use sex for your rebellion. You have a fine mind, Leckie, use your mind!

I set off down Broadway like I own the place. Funky Broadway, Broadway, New York, the city that never sleeps. On the bus I sit by the window, but pretty soon I give up my seat to an old lady. She looks like a raisin in a wig. She wears this mauve crochet dress, which is something to see. I can tell it required a lot of patience to make.

The bus lurches across the top of the park, 110th Street, there's a song about that too. There's a song about damn near every street in New York. I just love this park. Imagine it all being fake! The lakes and little hills and where the trees grow—somebody just made it up like a story. For a hundred years it's been here, kept up beautifully and everybody just enjoying the hell out of it, even though it is valuable real estate and there's not enough apartments to go around. They keep that park because everybody likes it and needs it there. Now that's the kind of thing that restores my faith in people. Even if people do get hurt and raped and killed sometimes and homeless people pee in the bushes and live under them and all that, it's still a nice park.

Down we go on the Museum Mile. It makes me feel important riding down Fifth Avenue on the Museum Mile. It's the grand scale of things. Big stone buildings and wide sidewalks on the left, and on the right the darker stone wall and Central Park beyond. On the left people going to get some culture and on the right people going to play. Doormen all dressed up over here, must be sweating to death in all that braid-encrusted dark cloth. On the other side, bums sleeping on the benches, still wearing winter coats. Spanish-speaking girls taking their babies to the park over here, and over there, the most dolled up old ladies in Chanel and Hermes and Gucci and other stuff so fancy you never even heard of it. Old as Methuselah, but just perfect from scarf to shoes to handbag, from soup to nuts; they haven't had a thing to do but look good in New York for eighty years. And internationally, too. You can picture these ladies in magazine ads. Mrs. Foxfur of Fifth Avenue. Looking good! New York, Paris, Milan. Mrs. Bigbucks. Stepping out in style. Newport, Monte Carlo, Buenos Aires.

The Metropolitan Museum of Art, monolith of culture, microcosm of man's creation. In seventh grade we took a field trip to the Smithsonian, but the only thing I remember about the whole weekend is that Troy Avery, a big boy with a head like a football, smashed another boy's face into the bus window and knocked his tooth out. Smeared blood all down the window and on the seat. The teacher tried to get the stain out with Kleenex and 7UP. Later I let the injured boy kiss me in the back of the bus, and I could taste the saltiness of blood in his mouth.

Inside the museum I march right past all that medieval stuff—those Virgin Marys with the dead-looking eyes like teenagers in a

Don't Do Drugs commercial. They give me the willies. Them and
their little baby Jesuses, wan as middle-aged salesmen, unlucky in
love, ill-nourished and cheap with money. Pinched all around, which
to my mind is not at all the way a Baby Jesus should look. If Baby Jesus, savior of the world, can't be fat and happy, who can?

I tell you where I'm headed. Straight for Decorative Arts of Europe.
Every time I'm here there is hardly a soul in Decorative Arts of Europe. I love the big rooms full of gaudy knickknacks, tall beds hung
with tapestry, yards and yards of rug. It's the grand scale. You could
fit twenty of my apartment into one of these rooms. You could fit
twenty people in one of those beds and just go for it. I can barely fit
into my bed. Hell, it's not even a bed. It's a cot of the kind they loan
out in motels to people with too many children. A damn cot saggy
as an old breast.

Why would somebody buy an entire room and have the whole
thing moved—chandeliers, paneling, wallpaper, fireplace, and all—
across an ocean, so that it could sit in the Metropolitan Museum of
Art for people in another time to look at?

I am being highly entertained by the decorative arts of Europe. I
am being informed and edified; I have plenty of time to blow. And
then I hear a man's voice saying, "You know you want to."

There's nobody in the room with me.

"You know you want me to right now."

"No, you're crazy."

They are just around the corner; if I reached around the wall, I'd
probably touch them.

"What about the guard?"

"He's two rooms back. It's fine."

"We could get arrested."

"Nobody even comes in here." *(giggle)* "Until now."

(in a serious tone) "Quit it, Bernard. I'm serious. I'm not doing this."

Bernard?

"Just let me touch you then. I'll touch you and you touch me."

(whining, but considering giving in) "Bernaaard."

My Bernard?

The girl giggles. Very faintly, a zipper. Faintly, breathing.

I want to turn the corner and surprise them, but the urge passes. Briefly I consider fleeing to some safely populated gallery like Impressionism or Armor or Egypt. Here comes the guard, walking down the long corridor at a slow, uninterested pace. He's cleaning his fingernails with a matchbook. He has that quiet authority of the uniform that says *Step back. Don't touch. Put away your flash bulb and your potato chips. You are at the Metropolitan Museum of Art, not the bowling alley.*

"You like that? Is that how you like it?"

I feel as if I am the one the guard is about to catch, all flagrante delicto, etcetera, etcetera. If I don't stop him, he will pass me right by and find God knows what! Naked people rolling around on a three-hundred-year-old bed like redneck honeymooners at the Days Inn.

"Excuse me," I say loudly, "I was wondering if you could tell me what that is over there." I point, directing his gaze across the room.

He shrugs, tucks away his matchbook. "I don't know anything about the Decorative Arts of Europe. Here, look on the sign. See, the numbers match with the diagram. Here you go. Says here that's a clock. Don't look like any clock I ever saw, but what do I know? I'm from Queens. I'm just a guard. That's my dumb luck. Now in musical instruments I could tell you something. I know a lot about those because I am a musician myself. Have you been to see those yet?"

"No," I say, relieved he's picking up the conversation. I don't hear the voices anymore.

"You never seen so many wacko instruments in your life. From all over the world, China, Japan, India," he counts off on his fingers.

Two girls are passing through; they are fashionable in that European braless way. The guard eyes their free-range breasts and gives up his geography recitation to direct the girls to a bathroom. Tawdry girls, without even a token appreciation for the decorative arts of their native Europe.

I look down the corridor behind me and catch sight of the couple hustling away. The girl's out in front, the boy is running as if to catch her.

Bernard? My Bernard?

I TRY TO follow them, but they are gone. The girl was wearing a camisole and black pants, just like me, she had dark hair like mine, she could have been me, I could have been her. That could have been me and sweet Bernard who has a picture of his cat over his computer and doesn't want me to get in trouble. If he asked me to jerk him off in the Decorative Arts of Europe, I would do it. But he didn't ask me.

I still have time before I'm supposed to meet Mr. Middle-Aged Man on the roof, so I head to the Temple of Dendur. I want to sit in that grand atrium and clear my mind.

When I push through the heavy doors, I'm surprised to see that it's raining out. Rain crashes down the enormous glass wall, and I can see people outside scurrying, huddling under umbrellas. I sit and watch the lightning jag across the sky. Children throw pennies into the moat. Tourists are taking pictures of their friends in front of the Temple, and I want to tell them that their pictures will never come out because it is raining. It's too dark. They won't come out; nothing ever comes out the way you think it will. Nothing ever goes right.

Could I drag an Egyptian temple across the sea to save it from flooding? Do I have the patience to crochet a dress or make chain mail from bottle caps? No. I can't teach anybody to tap-dance, the only thing I ever got from a celebrity was a form letter, and maybe I do look like a whore in this outfit. I will never save my father from a life of drudgery at the sock company; I will never impress my mother by feats of intellect. It is possible that I will end this day sleeping with a middle-aged man who'll be too drunk to get it up and too sad to care.

Where is my can-do spirit now?

The rain stops as quickly as it started. The glass wall of the atrium is beaded as an old evening dress, but after a few minutes, the beads begin to roll away one by one into oblivion. Umbrellas shake, become shy, and fold into themselves.

It is time to meet my dull lover on the rooftop. I begin to push my way across the museum to find the right elevator. What will happen once I reach the roof garden?

Scenario One: Old-fashioned romance

I find the right elevator and am dumped onto the steaming pavement. In one glance I can see that Mr. Middle-Aged Man is not here. I buy a Coke and walk over to the edge, survey the park, Cleopatra's Needle, the skyline in the haze. It is broiling hot and a beautiful city.

And then I see him. Down at the other end, there he is. My Mr. Middle-Aged Man. A wave of comfort passes over me. I am cheered to realize again how good-looking he is. I am proud of the maturity it takes to fuck a middle-aged man with lots of problems. But I wait; I let him search for me and find me, and when he finally sees me, he strides over, waving, carrying a drink, which I am sure is not the first of the day. We embrace and kiss.

Three possible endings:

A. Moderate happiness, despair, forgetting.
B. Immediate despair, forgetting.
C. Despair, with or without initial happiness, not forgetting—in fact, torturing myself for the rest of my life with the memory of a love that could never succeed. Permanent scarring manifested by inability to love again, do meaningful work, raise healthy children, own property, enjoy sex, make decisions, create art, or age gracefully.

Scenario Two: Even more old-fashioned romance

I find the right elevator and am dumped out onto the steaming pavement. In one glance I can see that Mr. Middle-Aged Man is not here. I buy a Coke and walk over to the edge, survey the park, Cleopatra's Needle, the skyline in the haze. It is broiling hot and a beautiful city.

And then I see him. My Bernard, sweating, drinking water, one foot up on the ledge as if he's going to climb up.

I stand behind him and whisper, "You know you want to."

He starts, turns, smiles.

We sit down together and begin to talk. I don't tell him I've been stood up; he doesn't tell me his date deserted him. I tell Bernard about my brother Peter who speaks Urdu, imitates birdcalls, and adopted a badly burned dog who hardly had a scrap of fur left.

Bernard smiles again his angelic smile. He knows I am full of shit.

I'm in love.

Three: Improbable chivalry

... yada yada yada ... broiling hot and a beautiful city. At one end of the roof stands Mr. Middle-Aged Man, at the other, My Bernard. They both see me, come to my side, glare at each other, and begin to fight. I am horrified and thrilled by their passion for me. Their hatred of each other is so great that one of them, I can't decide which, ends up throwing the other one off the roof and impaling him on Cleopatra's Needle.

Far-fetched, but you have to admit it's pretty funny.

Four: Magic realism

... broiling hot and a beautiful city. There is no one on the rooftop that I recognize. Will I never find love? Don't I deserve love?

Then I see him. He is floating above the trees of the park, free form, with a little haze around him. Peter, more wonderful and brotherly than even I had imagined him, giving me the peace sign with one hand and flipping me off with the other. He alights on the ledge of the roof as softly as a tiny bird. A deeply spiritual conversation, possibly even a conversion of some sort, ensues.

THIS IS WHAT amazes me about the human brain—between the time it takes me to get from an atrium that houses an Egyptian temple that was drug across an ocean to a garden built on the roof of a museum in the most important city in the world—in that little bit of time, I have thought up, like, fifty possibilities for what could happen in the next ten minutes.

I stop and think about that for a minute. I mean literally. I stop so fast and stand so dumb, so sore amazed as they say in the Bible, that a lady bumps into me. She doesn't even say excuse me.

Amazing.

I'M SURE YOU know what happens. People like you always know. You have a way of guessing correctly. Me, I never know jack. I don't know what's going to happen and when it does, I don't know why. That doesn't mean I don't have any hopes or expectations or whatever (though I'm beginning to see why some people give them up), it just means I don't pretend to know what's going to happen. I just guess what might happen. I just think about what I would *like* to happen.

I find the right elevator and am dumped onto the steaming pavement. I buy a Coke and walk over to the edge, survey the park, Cleopatra's Needle, the skyline in the haze. It is broiling hot and a beautiful city.

Sex Romp Gone Wrong

The doctor told Liza to keep track on her calendar or her phone. The doctor didn't have a thirteen-year-old daughter going through her purse, searching for money and gum and private information. Liza decided to use a code.

Regular :)

Kinky ;)

Oral : P

Angry >: |

If Bill had not shaved :{

Orgasmic @$%#*

For a few weeks, Liza's calendar notations resembled the text messages Grace sent to her best friend Nicola. In bed with Bill, Liza started mixing things up, just so she could record the night with a new symbol. Bill didn't know what had gotten into her, but he was all for it. Gradually, though, as with most things, the charm wore off, and the calendar went back to showing school events, deadlines, when to give the dog his heartworm pill. No smileys. Nothing that looked like irate Sarge giving Beetle Bailey the business.

Liza preferred to think of the symbols not as emoticons but as a shorthand inspired by William Byrd. Back in colonial Virginia, Byrd found the time: "I rogered my wife in the morning and also wrote a letter to England and settled several accounts." William Byrd didn't have to worry about laundry and PTA meetings and driving his mother to the store.

WHEN SCHOOL LET out for summer, Liza decided to get serious again about trying. She looked at the calendar and realized that her next ovulation coincided with one of Bill's horrible IT conventions, a Thursday and Friday night, three hours away by car. He was getting a hotel room anyway, so Liza figured what the heck. She would go along, and they would :), maybe : P, and, with any luck at all, @$%#! Grace could stay the two nights with Liza's mother.

Then her mother got sick—fever, antibiotics. Grace begged to go to Nicola's, but Liza couldn't stomach that. The father a write-off, the mother working late nights in a restaurant, with a new boyfriend every few months. Bill didn't want to pay for a second hotel room for Grace, but the doctor had said *every day*. That meant Liza would have to figure out how to get Grace out of the room for a little while. Liza had to do all the thinking about it, the scheduling, the keeping track. Bill just sat at his computer or played with his phone until she said it was time.

The first night, there was a sit-down dinner. Keynote: Cyber Blah Blah of the Future. Most of the other guys had not brought wives. By the looks of them, Liza doubted they had volunteers, of any gender, for sexual or domestic congress. In the world of IT, Bill was an Adonis. Liza drunk-doodled dirty pictures on her napkin until Bill suggested she put down the pen and stop with the vodka tonics. Grace snubbed the entree, ate the dessert, then slumped over like she'd been shot and started texting away, her thumbs working like little pistons. A lot of the guys in the banquet hall were doing the same, holding their devices down in their laps in a lame effort to hide what they were doing. Up in the room later, Bill laughed when Liza said she *hoped* that's what those guys were doing with their hands under the tables.

Grace got in the second double bed and turned on a movie. Needless to say, there was no @$%&* that night. Not even a :).

: (

THE NEXT MORNING Bill cleaned his glasses, filled his breast pocket with new business cards, and said he was going down early to network over coffee and Danish before the first panel session.

"Bill, you look just as shiny as a new penny." Liza blew him a kiss from the bed, then hummed a few bars of "Afternoon Delight" to remind him that they had an appointment later in the day. She planned to send Grace down to the pool at 1:45; he was to come back to the room at 2:00 for half an hour of the best he ever had. He gave her a thumbs-up to show he understood. The thumbs-up was a turnoff Liza was used to overlooking.

"Don't y'all want to come down and get some free breakfast?" he said. "It's free."

Grace groaned from the other bed, huddled under the twisted covers so all they could see was some brown hair on the pillow. "Free breakfasts suck."

"Ah," said Bill, winking at Liza. "They don't have to taste good when they're free."

"That's *why* they're free," Liza added.

After Bill left, Grace went back to sleep. The floor was covered with clothes, the chest of drawers littered with free local magazines from the hotel lobby and the cheese popcorn they'd been passing around in the car the day before, but Liza wasn't about to tidy. What a treat to have no house to clean, no dog to walk, no papers to grade. She picked up her biography of Samuel Pepys and read that an operation for kidney stones may have left him unable to get his wife pregnant. His wife was only fourteen when they married, so it wasn't like her age was the problem. At girls' nights, over wine, Liza's friends prated optimistically about how forty was the new thirty. She called their bullshit, reminded them that living longer meant more old age, not more youth. Look already at our cracking knees, our gray hairs, our saggy bits, she'd say. Recall our regretful, mourning hearts; our ancient, uncooperative eggs. At least you have one child, her childless friends said. They were trying so hard: spending money, counting days, taking temperatures, swallowing the sickening pills, injecting themselves, enduring the compulsory sex. Everybody screamed, thrilled, when one of them succeeded, but at the baby shower somebody always cried in the bathroom while the gifts were being opened.

Grace woke again, picked up the book she'd brought, and got into bed with Liza. Sometimes they still did this at home, lying close together under the covers, reading, knowing better than to ruin it with talking. After a while, Grace said she was hungry.

"How about some room service?" Liza said.

"Yessss." Grace offered a fist bump, her gold standard of affection. When Liza saw the menu prices, she knew Bill would have a fit, but she let Grace call the order down anyway. As they waited for the food, Grace switched on the TV and raced through the channels. She paused when a familiar series of images flashed across the scene—Li'l KrayZ's video for her inescapably catchy hit "I Don't Have to Tell You." Liza caught herself singing it sometimes, even though she loathed everything Li'l KrayZ represented. A recent supermarket tabloid had blazoned *KrayZ's Sex Romp Gone Wrong!* over a picture in which the girl looked much puffier than she did on television.

Grace cranked the volume and danced in front of the TV.

I don't have to tell you
What you already KNOW
I'm Li'l KrayZ
And I'm sex-y
And you ain't gettin' none.

Up until this point in the video, a pack of loitering boys had been catcalling and pantomiming what they wanted to do to her, but now they could only writhe in an agony of rejection as KrayZ curled her lip, shook her head, and sashayed down the street, her hips swinging like a bell on a holy day.

Grace hopped to the side and shimmied in imitation of KrayZ's backup dancers, her fanny wiggling without mercy in her pink pajamas. What choice did the boys have but to give chase like wild dogs?

"Turn that down, please."

Now that Grace was thirteen, strangers no longer asked Liza if she was going to have another baby—each time they'd said it, as the years went by and no second child appeared, like a blow. Liza's friends with children Grace's age said she was crazy to want another. They assumed she'd forgotten the limbo hours at the pediatrician's, the pharmacy, the supermarket, the Stride Rite, everything taking longer than it ought and maybe never getting done at all. But she hadn't forgotten. When Grace was a baby and Liza was newly married, older women would tell her how the baby stage would go so fast, and then her sweet baby would grow into a money-stealing slut who would show Bill and Liza how much she hated them by smoking drugs and wrecking cars. She would smile and nod, petting Grace, never confessing how bored she was, that she hadn't imagined how whole hours could exist inside each minute of crying, of painful nursing, of slobbery demands for attention.

In a way, of course, the old women had been right. Bill finished his graduate degree and got a good job. Grace started school. Liza returned to teaching. Time righted itself, then accelerated. Life did seem to go by faster now, and it wasn't as full of surprises as it had once been. Some of the old hurts—once so sharp—no longer bothered Liza, and new troubles brought a pain at once deeper and easier to accept. After all, it was her job as a history teacher to show students that you could look down the whole long sweep of time and see the cycles of calamity and boom, how things change and repeat.

Naturally, her students thought she was Methuselah. Every time they mentioned something she hadn't heard of—some TV star, band, video game, website—some juvenile crap—they dismissed her. Old. How could she know? *Yeah?* she wanted to say. *I'm old, but I know things, you little fuckers.* Sometimes she said it, without the *fuckers*, to Grace, who was going into ninth grade in the fall, one more year to go until the grade Liza taught. Way past the age when she would write her mother love notes and cry, "I'm lonely!" as she banged on Liza's locked bathroom door. Now Liza was the one who passed Grace's closed door and wanted to pound on it until she was taken in. She wanted to go back to the beginning, to that snug bundle in her arms, the new hand touching her face as though it held the key to the universe.

AT 1:30, LIZA TOLD Grace to get her bathing suit on. She tried to be patient as Grace changed her hair, applied lip gloss, and tried on three different outfits over her new lime green bikini. Grace had grinned in the store when Liza told her not to let her father see it; it was worrisome how much the child loved to conspire. By 1:55, Grace settled on shorts and a t-shirt over the bikini. Flip-flops, electric blue toenails, long brown hair curling at her shoulders, pale skin glowing, breasts perky—she looked at least sixteen. Slightly panicked, Liza looked out the window and was relieved to see only a mother and two preschoolers in the pool.

"Aren't you coming?" Grace asked.

"You go on. I'll come down in a bit. I just want to call your grandmother and see how she's doing."

The room had been cleaned earlier when they'd moseyed out for window-shopping and falafel, but Grace had torn it up again in the hour they'd been back. Quickly, Liza stuffed Grace's clothes back into her duffel bag, careful not to look what else might be in there. At home, she didn't clean Grace's room anymore because she was afraid of finding her diary. She'd seen enough of her texts to Nicola to know she didn't want to see anything more detailed.

2:02. She brushed her hair and sniffed under her arms, even though she'd showered that morning. Bill's shaving things and Grace's makeup littered the bathroom counter—including an eye-shadow Liza had never seen before (two alarming shades, Bruise and Regret). She tried it—too dark—then washed it off. Bill ought to be up any second. She checked out the window again. Grace was spreading her towel on a lounge chair, but now, in addition to the mother and children, there was a man. Liza didn't trust his slick hair, bulky arms, and virile mustache. She thought she might have to go down there and sit with Grace, but then he was joined by a tan bottle blond in a fuchsia tank, and Liza could tell from seven stories up that the blond wasn't going to let the virile mustache look at another female. She could tell from seven stories up that they were the kind of people who called women *females*.

Liza closed the curtains, stripped, got under the sheet, and watched the alarm clock count off its red numbers. By 2:16, she knew that even if he came, there was no way she'd get past her anger quickly enough to do what they needed to do in the time allotted. At 2:19, she went fetal and indulged in a brief cry. When it was over, she lay staring at the framed poster of white horses on a beach and the brassy lamps with the on-off buttons at their bases like weird little nipples. Once upon a time, the impersonality of hotel rooms had excited her; anything might happen in them. Now the place's emptiness annihilated her, and she had to sit up just so she could see Grace's bag and Bill's pajama shirt draped over the back of the chair.

On the rare occasions when her husband and daughter went away together overnight, she relished not having to cook or find their misplaced things or listen to their same-old, same-old. Invariably, though, as night fell, she'd fret. She'd call them, calming as soon as she heard their voices, feeling silly to have worried. But then the call would end, and as the night wore on and it grew too late, too ridiculous, to call again, the idea would overtake her that they had somehow never existed, that she had made them up. *Oh, stop it*, she'd tell herself as she brushed her teeth and got into bed. Look at their stuff everywhere. They're real. Of course they are. She'd read until very late, leaving the lamp on because in the dark she'd just upset herself again.

2:22. If only Bill would come to the room *right that minute*, she'd be so glad to see him that she wouldn't even be angry.

2:25. She washed her face, put on her black tankini and cover-up, and went down to the pool. The oiled tan couple lay on their loungers, holding hands, eyes closed, as though their glistening required concentration. A dozen college kids splashed on the other side of the pool, dunking each other and laughing. Grace, head bent over her book, still hadn't taken off her t-shirt.

"Don't you want to go in?" Liza dipped her toe in the water. "Cool off?"

"Not right now," Grace muttered.

"Well, I don't know why I got you that new suit if you're not going to swim."

Grace flounced off the chair, tore off her shirt, and dropped into the water. After a few furious laps, she climbed out, shoulders hunched forward, and quickly wrapped herself in her towel. Hair dripping, she glared at her mother.

"Happy?"

GRASSY STRIPS SEPARATED the rows of cars, and a dirty pink light fondled the unfamiliar cityscape. Grace gazed out the plateglass window at the empty pool and the steaming parking lot. She ate one of the fries from her room-service plate and texted Nicola: Soooo brd! Gng 2 bar!

Her parents hadn't said she couldn't go out of the room, but she knew they expected her not to from the way her mother had said, "Don't stay up too late," and "Don't open the door for anybody," and "You'll be okay here, won't you?" Grace had a plan, though. She knew her parents would drink several sweating glasses of pinot grigio with their dinner, which would take a long time, so she'd just make sure she got back upstairs before they did.

She glanced at the TV. She was hoping "I Don't Have to Tell You" would come on again so she could dance all out, grindier this time now that her mother wasn't there to see. The second verse was the best:

> I don't have to tell you
> I need a man with class
> Baby, you gotta know
> It takes more than dough
> To get a piece of this ass!

Here Grace and Nicola always shouted: *ASS!* In the video when KrayZ did this line she pouted and rubbed her butt like she was polishing it.

Grace put on her makeup and stared at herself. The eyeshadow didn't look right, so she wiped most of it off until her eyelids looked only vaguely dark—like maybe she'd been punched a few weeks ago—but also kind of mysterious. She played "I Don't Have to Tell You" on her phone and sang to the mirror:

> *I'm Li'l Grace-Z*
> *And I'm SEX-y.*

She rifled through her old duffel bag with the enormous dumb bumblebee on the side that she'd had since she was, like, eight or something. Crushed in the bottom, she found the purple halter that she'd bought with Nicola the last time her mom had dropped them off at the mall. It had been marked down to only $7.99, a real bargain and just like something Li'l KrayZ would wear.

"That's too revealing," her mother would say if she saw it. Her father would close his eyes, put his hand to the side of his head, and pretend to be having a stroke.

Her phone buzzed. Nicola: At movies.

Of course. Out with that idiot, her new boyfriend.

Grace: Dont do anything I wouldnt LOL ;)

Nicola: U mean nothing? : P

Grace: Ha ha.

She put on her mother's high-heeled sandals and walked back into the bathroom. Taller, she felt she could do anything. When she was grown, she planned to be a dancer and then a lawyer. She wondered if Ruth Bader Ginsburg wore heels under her judicial robes. Grace might go into patent law because she liked inventions. They'd gotten a pair of orange kittens when she was six, brother and sister, and she'd named them Tesla and Alva. Her dad hated Tesla because he always peed in front of his chair. Alva was the sweetie. Oh, suddenly she missed the kitties! Well, she'd see them tomorrow and give them a majillion kisses to make up for being gone.

She braided her hair Pocahontas style and put rubberbands around the ends. That was the way KrayZ wore her hair in the video for her earlier hit, "Bump All Night." Grace wished her hair was blond, or at least red, but there was nothing she could do about it because her mother didn't believe in dying hair. Her mom had all these rules that were mostly ways to treat Grace like a baby, but then, Nicola said, that was a schoolteacher for ya. Nicola's mom didn't have time to make any rules, but she did make Nicola babysit her brother a lot, which Nicola said was making her old before her time, which was why she smoked. Grace had tried cigarettes with Nicola, but they were too disgusting. "We could try weed instead," Nicola had said, but when she saw Grace's face, she said, "Just kidding." Knowing Nicola, though, it would come up again, and Grace wasn't sure yet what she would do.

Her dad had a secret pack of Marlboros hidden in his computer bag. Grace wondered whether he smoked weed sometimes, too. He wasn't supposed to smoke anything, not just because it was unhealthy and a bad example for Grace but because it would lower his sperm count. She'd overheard her mom telling him that if their luck didn't change soon, they would have to decide whether to take "more dire measures." Nicola liked to gross her out by talking about how Grace's dad would go in a room at the doctor's and jerk off in a Dixie cup while he looked at porn.

"Your mom has to wait in another room for the nurse to come put your dad's jizz into her with a syringy thing."

"I know! Shut up!"

Nicola thought she had to teach Grace everything because she was the one who'd told her about doggy style and going down. The computer at Nicola's house didn't have all those blocks that Grace's dad had put on her laptop. That was how they'd found out the particulars of Li'l KrayZ's three-way with her personal trainer and coked-out former child star Cody Blaine. Even before the whole story came out, Nicola correctly predicted that it was Cody who had leaked the video because his career was tanking so bad he'd take any kind of publicity. Nicola understood a lot about motives and human nature.

Grace made her face serious like the old white-haired guy in the movie of *Inherit the Wind* that they had watched in English class. Leaning toward the mirror, she pounded her fist on the bathroom counter and declaimed, "Because fanaticism and ignorance is forever busy, and needs feeding! And soon, your honor, with banners flying and with drums beating, we'll be marching backward! Backward! Through the glorious ages of that sixteenth century when bigots burned the man who dared bring enlightenment and intelligence to the human mind!"

It had struck Grace that middle school was not unlike that sixteenth century or, for that matter, the monkey trials themselves. Try floating a new idea in eighth grade, or being different. Nicola complained that it was too obvious—the play, and why the teacher had them reading it. "It makes sense that you like it, though, since you want to be a lawyer." Something about the way Nicola pronounced the word *lawyer* made Grace feel she didn't approve of her chosen profession.

Her braids looked stupid, so she undid them and brushed her hair back to its normal style. Maybe the high heels with shorts were what her grandmother would call "trying too hard." She changed into her sneakers and looked at herself again. Nicola had sworn the purple halter looked good, even if Grace didn't quite fill it out yet. If Grace didn't buy it, Nicola was going to since it was such a steal. But now Grace remembered the pool that afternoon, how she'd felt too naked in her bikini around those college kids, many of them guys, some of them hot. She took off the halter, stuffed it back into her duffel, and put on a bra and shirt. Now she felt normal, except that she was about to go to a hotel bar, alone.

She slid her key card into her pocket as the door swung shut behind her with a bump and a click. In the airless hallway, room-service trays littered the carpet, smelling like school lunch. Alone on the ride down, she practiced a couple of Li'l KrayZ's steps and made the elevator rock. The cavernous lobby had impressed her at check-in yesterday, but now, as she crossed the buffed marble floor with what she hoped looked like nonchalance, even world-weariness, she barely glanced at the plant-encircled fountain or the plush, over-sized chairs. She had a mission: spying on her parents through the restaurant's open doors.

It was early, and the waiters stood around in their black shirts, waiting for customers. Her parents' was the only table with a lit candle. They didn't have their food yet, just the wine. Her mom's back was to the door, and she was gesturing wildly the way she did when telling a story, making her dad laugh. Nicola said Grace was lucky her parents didn't have boyfriends and girlfriends. Grace was glad about that, though she had noticed that kids with divorced parents had nicer phones and later curfews.

Music started nearby—a mouse-faced woman in an ankle-length skirt mournfully sawed away at a cello. Her long, straight hair was held back from her face by one big barrette, the same way Grace's ex–best friend Jessica wore hers. She didn't hate Jessica now or anything; it was just that they'd gone different ways since sixth grade. Grace was looking toward the future, while Jessica was still filling her notebooks with drawings of horses and unicorns. Last fall a bully had stuck a bloody pad to the door of Jessica's locker, right on the handle, and all day long she'd gotten in trouble for not having her books in class. Now, when people called her Maxi or asked if she had wings, Jessica never said anything, just looked sick and turned away. Grace wished she could help her somehow, but Nicola said you couldn't do much for a person with no gumption.

Grace crossed the lobby again and went into the bar. The place was decorated to look old-timey—lots of dark wood, brass railings, glass-globed lights etched with a cursive word: *O'Dooligans*, maybe? She wouldn't wear her glasses except when her mom made her or she was alone. They were so old lady. The frames she wanted had cost $390, and her mother had just shook her head and pointed to

the bargain rack. Grace was never sure if her parents were poor or
just cheap.

She sat on one of the stools and put down her phone. The bartender set a napkin in front of her.

"What'll you have? A martini? Maybe a double?"

God, what a dick. He was like a dad or something. Not like her dad,
who was nice, but one of those dick dads. Pudgy, with thinning beige
hair and rat eyes, he was like the doofus neighbor on a sitcom. Like
one of those doofus neighbor dick dads on a show where the kids
were also total dicks and doofuses. She wanted to ask him weren't
bartenders supposed to have some charm? Instead, she mumbled
that she'd like a Coke. He brought it, then went back to the end of the
bar, crossed his arms, and looked up at the TV hanging on the wall.
Now and then he said something to an old man in a suit who was
drinking brown liquor. He was probably dicky, too. She didn't know if
they were sharing their opinions about the news or what. She didn't
care. The news was boring, and this bar was boring. She didn't know
what she had thought would be fun about it. She should've stayed in
her room instead of wasting her money on an overpriced Coke and
risking getting in trouble with her parents.

Four men came in, obviously from the same convention as her father. Her mother said you could always tell IT guys by their deathly
pallor and their sparkling small talk. When they passed her, carrying
their beers to a table, one of them winked at her, trying to be funny.
At least some guys could be nice.

"Excuse me," said a voice behind her. She turned around on her stool.

OMG, she would text Nicola later—HOT!!!!!! One of the college guys from the pool that afternoon: long brown hair, dark eyes, tan. He wore a red polo and reminded her of the soccer players at her school, with their lazy faces and fit bodies.

"Can I sit here?"

"Knock yourself out." This was a line her father liked to say.

He sat down and lifted his hand to signal the bartender.

"I saw you at the pool today." He finished sending a text, then set his phone down and looked at her. He had pretty eyelashes and straight, white teeth. Pretty boy, she'd tell Nicola.

"With your sister, maybe?"

"That was my mom."

"Oh, really? Y'all, like, on a shopping trip or something?"

He was kind of dumb, but she guessed that didn't really matter.

"No, my dad has a conference here in the hotel. We just came to hang out."

"Oh, that's cool." He looked toward the bartender. "Why the fuck doesn't that guy come over here?"

"That guy's a dick," said Grace, sipping her Coke.

"I'm Tom, by the way." He turned to look at her again. What an easy smile he had. Their knees were almost touching under the bar, and now she noticed his necklace, a rawhide with a black shark's tooth that sat in the depression at the base of his throat.

"Grace," she said, putting out her hand. Instantly, she wondered if that was a dumb thing to do, but she felt reassured when he happily shook it. His hand was warm, his grip solid.

"Sweet to meet you, Grace." He said it as though he liked the rhyme, as though it was something he'd said to girls before.

The bartender came over now, wiping his hands on his apron.

"What do you have on draft?" Tom asked.

The bartender sighed. "Son, let me see your ID."

So rude, Grace would tell Nicola. Like his job is *hard*.

Tom pulled a wallet out of his back pocket and flipped it open. The bartender glanced at the license, then waved it away. Looking up at the television again, he reeled off the beer names.

"Dos Equis," Tom said.

When the bartender went off to the taps at the other end of the bar, Tom said, "Jeez. He give you a hard time like that?"

"Kind of. But it's pretty obvious I'm not twenty-one."

"How old are you?"

"I'm going to be a freshman next year."

"Oh? Where?"

"What?"

"Where are you going to college?"

"Tulane," Grace said, naming the first college that popped into her head.

"That's going to be awesome! Partying in N'awlins for four freaking years! You are going to have such a good time. I mean, State is awesome, too, but New Orleans!"

He told her he was at the hotel with his friends because one of his old roommates from State was getting married the next day. Could she believe that shit? Dude just graduated three weeks ago and now he was getting freaking *married?* Tom shook his head in sad disbelief. His beer came, which seemed to cheer him up, and he asked her what she was into, if she played any sports, if she had a boyfriend. It surprised her how smoothly she lied, how easily he believed that she was dating, driving, experienced. It helped that he wasn't as awkward as guys her age; it also helped that he wasn't too bright. For a real boyfriend, she'd want somebody much smarter, of course, but Tom was just fine for now. What he lacked in intelligence, he made up for with good looks and his advanced age. He was providing exactly what she had come to O'Dooligans in search of—experience—and his dumbness would just be another funny detail of the story she couldn't wait to tell Nicola: how she'd picked up a certifiable hottie in a hotel bar.

"A bunch of us are going swimming. You want to go?"

"Sure."

It was okay that there were other people in the elevator when they went upstairs. She wasn't quite ready to be alone with him. Later, in the pool, she hoped Tom might kiss her. This spring she'd let a boy kiss her at the school dance—just as an experiment because the boy she really liked had brought another girl—and the fact of having done it turned out to be more exciting than the actual kiss, which was fairly disgusting.

When they got to her room, she made Tom wait in the hall while she put her damp suit back on, wiggled into her shorts and shirt, checked her makeup. Her cheeks were flushed. Was she pretty? She didn't know. She scribbled a quick note: *Gone swimming.* Her mother was going to kill her.

They went down two floors. As soon as they stepped off the elevator, Grace could feel the bass thumping along the floor. Down the hall, the noise grew louder, and by the time they reached room 523, Grace heard screams of laughter coming from inside.

"Sounds like they're getting crazy." Tom grinned like that was a good thing and knocked. Before Grace could ask why didn't they just go straight to the pool, a burly, bearded guy in a Steelers shirt hustled them in and stuffed a towel along the bottom of the door. Music was pounding in the dim, smoky room, and the only light was coming from the television, a few phones, and the bathroom, where a girl was already passed out under the sink, her hair spread across her face. Tom stepped over the girl's feet and pulled the last beer out of the melting ice in the tub, then guided Grace toward the first bed. People grudgingly moved so they could sit. On the second bed, three girls danced, bouncing the people sitting around the edges. At the table by the window, guys took turns hitting each other's knuckles with a deck of cards, roaring in triumph or pain when they hit or got hit.

Tom put his arm around Grace and offered his beer. It was weak and bitter and not very cold. The red-eyed girl next to her shouted in her ear. "Where the hell did Tom find you? How old are you, anyway?"

"Seventeen."

"My ass." The girl blew a thin stream of blue smoke and turned away. Grace gripped the beer as Tom pulled her closer. He put his mouth to her ear, muttering words she couldn't understand, then rubbed the side of her breast with one hand. His other hand ran slowly up her leg, wandering a finger into her inseam. Holding the beer in one hand and her phone in the other, she froze, hoping the mean-eyed girl did not turn back to look. She wished he would wait until they went down to the pool, away from all these people, but he was already putting his mouth on her neck, and she couldn't help thinking of an octopus she'd once seen at the aquarium, his bulbous head and tentacles pale and urgent against the glass.

It was at this kind of party that Nicola confessed she had once gone farther than she wanted to with two guys in a car. It wasn't Nicola's way to admit that anybody could force her to do anything, but then best friends didn't always have to explain everything to each other.

The burly doorkeeper let in two more guys. "Back from the hunt!" they shouted, holding up plastic tubing and two cases of beer. The room welcomed them with happy cheers, and a group followed the hunters into the bathroom. Tom followed, too. Soon there were profane hollers, then a chant: *Go, go, go!*

Grace pushed her way out of the room and ran toward the elevator. Again and again, she mashed the button, trying to think what she would say if Tom came after her and suggested they go somewhere quieter. Half hoping, half afraid, she thought of the beer on his breath and how she wouldn't know how to stop his hands going where she wasn't ready for them to go.

The elevator doors slid open. Inside, a man and a woman were kissing. It took a minute for Grace to see they were her parents, going at it like it was nuclear winter and any minute the sun was going to be blocked out for good.

Hot Lesbian
Vampire Magic School

A Ballet in Three Acts, story by Lucy Tisdale

(Carly—once you write the music, we'll add "score by Carly Jackson")

Act I, scene 1: The great hall

Carly—Opening music should be sprightly but with an eerie edge befitting the magical atmosphere and also giving A Portent of Things to Come

Through a high window a full white moon is visible. The hall is lined with stately looking coffins. A grand buffet is laid on a long table, above which the arched ceiling is hung with red banners depicting various magical symbols, like ankh, magic eye, pentagram . . .

these should def. be <u>REAL</u> magical symbols, not just some fake-ass made-up bullshit

Two dozen superhot girls mill about the stage, eating, drinking, talking, laughing. They are dressed in form-fitting black unitards and capes of varying lengths and colors depending on their school rank.

Suddenly, the music stops. The toll of a clock is heard. The students freeze, some with wands raised in anticipation of trouble. At each stroke of the clock, a coffin opens, and the teachers emerge, one by one, and take their seats upon the dais at the top of the stage. The last to emerge, at the stroke of midnight, is the headmistress, Patricia, who ascends the dais imperiously.

She waves her wand over the group of older girls in the longest capes. They dance, demonstrating to the new students some of the wonderful things they will learn in the coming year, such as: transforming people into animals, causing people to disappear, sucking blood, then causing the sucked-out people to disappear. At the end of the dance, the new girls pair off and begin to leave the stage. The spotlight picks out first Lucretia Thibodeaux and then Clarie Jacquesfils. They gaze at each other as if under a SPELL.

Act I, scene 2: Lucretia and Clarie's tower room

Lucretia and Clarie kneel facing each other on the bed. (There are also two coffins leaning against the wall for them to sleep in. The bed is for SEX.) The moonlight falls between them, illuminating their bare breasts. They talk—

Ok, from here on, if I say they talk, that means they pantomime, and the music has to fit the stuff they're acting out.

—they talk to each other about their homes—Lucretia's cold succubus of a mother, Clarie's evil wizard grandfather, the unfairness of life and how thankful they are to have come to a place where they, as hot teenage lesbian vampire magicians, can finally be themselves.

They dance a joyous pas de deux, and as the first heart-breaking sunray slices into the room, they share a passionate tongue kiss, then climb into their coffins to rest.

Act II, scene 1: A graveyard

Energetic music. The new girls are doing gym in the graveyard. (They wear old-style sweatbands around their foreheads to show that they are getting hot and sweaty.) As they do sit-ups on the slab graves and use the tombstones for pushups, Marcella, a big, not-hot (how did she get into this school?) second-year BITCH, shimmies up a ten-foot-high obelisk and perches on the top, *en pointe, en arabesque*, even, before leaping off, landing right next to an admiring Clarie. Marcella flexes her muscles for Clarie, and they laugh together while Lucretia looks on in a RAGE.

Finally, able to stand it no longer, Lucretia rushes at Marcella. They fight. Lucretia Thibodeaux reveals herself to be especially wild and hot-tempered, even among the already wild and hot-tempered population of hot teenage lesbian vampire magicians, and she is kicking some booTAY. Laissez your bons temps roulee, my friend—go ahead, Lucretia seems to be saying. I will find a way to fuck it up with some serious craziness.

There is a heated dance battle.

Music should have a back-and-forth quality because first Lucretia will show her stuff and then Marcella, and then Lucretia will do some more amazing moves, and then Marcella, etc., etc., the dancing just getting more and more awesome but then by the end they are doing actual hand-to-hand combat and the music has to be INTENSE.

Just as it seems Lucretia will choke Marcella to death, Clarie desperately waves her wand. Because she is inexperienced and doesn't know how to control her magic yet, Lucretia is only half transformed and now has a cat's head, paws, and tail but her own body. Though weirdly she is *hotter than ever* like this, Lucretia doesn't like it. In her distress, she leaps and bounds about the stage (lots of awkward pas de chats, naturally, as that is the step of the CAT), begging the other girls to return her to her regular form. But either they don't know how or they are afraid to anger Marcella, who is now putting her arm around Clarie like she fucking owns her or something, like somebody can *own* another person. Clarie looks sorrowfully back over her shoulder as she exits with Marcella, stage right.

Act II, scene 2: The dorm common room

Girls are lying around on the sofas in sweatpants, looking not so hot and eating pizzas and chocolate candies. Lucretia is with them, having been restored to her usual form by one of the teachers. Boxes of pads and tampons lie around to show that they are all on their period, which can happen sometimes when a bunch of women/girls live all together in one place—

Oh God! The PMS at this school, you cannot even—it would burn your brain to cinders to even imagine it.

—then they get up and all perform an ensemble dance, at first sluggish, then ramping up into dervishdom, to demonstrate the mad mood swings of people on PERIODS.

At the climax of the dance, stupid Marcella rushes in, panicked! Clarie is missing!!

Everybody freezes in horror.

Then they all start whispering and pointing their fingers at Lucretia, who looks like: What? Who, me? Oh. No. You. Didn't. Just. Point. *A moi!*

Act III, scene 1: Lucretia and Clarie's tower room

Lucretia weeps alone on her bed. She is devastated that Clarie is missing and cannot believe that anybody would think she was behind it in any way. Clarie's magic cape is still hanging on a hook on the wall, and Lucretia takes it down and hugs it to her breast and floats about the room, her every pirouette and developpé an exquisite manifestation of her deep grief. Gradually, as her sadness begins to weigh upon her so heavily that she can no longer dance, she collapses against the bookshelf at the side of the room. It suddenly swings away from her. It is a secret bookcase door opening on a HIDDEN PASSAGE! Lucretia ties on Clarie's cape for courage.

BTW, I still have your hoodie you left at my house last time you slept over.

Lucretia begins to climb the secret stair as the music crescendos ominously.

Act III, scene 2: Headmistress Patricia's chamber

Lucretia steps up into a stone-walled chamber. It is very very magical looking. Patricia sits writing in a large ledger at an ornately carved desk, looking sage in a wizard hat and sexy glasses. She has been expecting Lucretia, who sobs that she had nothing to do with Clarie's disappearance. *I love her,* she pleads, literally on her knees. Patricia closes her eyes and nods like she is telling herself, *Patience, Patricia.* Patience with these young and wayward and wild, and none more young and wayward and wild than brave young Thibodeux here.

I love her! Lucretia sobs again, slightly calmer, as she blows into the enormous black hanky Patricia has handed her.

Patricia sits back in her chair and tents her fingers and slits her eyes and shows the tips of her fangs in a weary way. She says, as Headmistress of Hot Lesbian Vampire Magic School, do you think I can't *tell* when two girls seriously dig each other?

Lucretia bows her head. She has been schooled and feels defeated, like maybe what she and Clarie shared was kind of—well, ordinary.

But it so wasn't, was it, Carly? Or isn't? Was or is?

Two vampires together is a doomed relationship, Patricia demonstrates in a sad dance of warning. Ultimately, it cannot work. What are you going to do, suck each other's blood, back and forth, forever?

Lucretia says, yes, exactly! Sit down, and I will show you. She dances a lovely solo, twirling Clarie's cape, embracing it, wrapping it around herself, showing what a beautiful synergy that would be, two young hot lesbian vampires loving each other, like an amazing Möbius strip of blood-sucking never-ending. We wouldn't even have names anymore. We'd be like the artist formerly known as, you know. We would the two of us together just be an infinity symbol.

—the music here should repeat but build, repeat but build, it should sound like a long, slow night of loving. The dance will be very sensual but not just in a dirty humpy way because that's not all this relationship is about, it is a SOUL thing, I know you know what I mean—

Patricia admires her passion but shakes her head. It can never be. Clarie's parents have transferred her to another school.

Lucretia clutches her chest as though she has had a stake driven through her heart. Why do you put all us hot lesbian vampires in here together if you don't want us to *love* each other? she shouts, sweeping her arm across one of Patricia's shelves and sending some magical stuff crashing to the floor, producing plumes of red and silver smoke.

Patricia shakes her head with bored regret. How many times has she had this same conversation? You are here to learn magic, my dear, not love.

The music becomes mournful, ethereal. Lucretia dances over to the window. She stares out, wondering where her love, her Clarie, has gone. She pictures a grim future of trolling coffeehouses and Ala-teen meetings for quick sex and easy blood. She sees that there is NO MAGIC without love. Ignoring Patricia's cries, she steps onto the window ledge and leaps into the void.

But, just as all seems lost, the wind lifts Clarie's enchanted cape, and Lucretia soars higher, fated to fly forever above the mist.

CURTAIN

Flown

W endy can't help hovering outside the den when her fourteen-year-old daughter Megan's older friend Harris first comes over to play video games on a Saturday. They're talking about a woman named Cora Goodnight who's all over the local news for (probably) killing her three husbands and her pastor. The church directory photo posted with each telling of her story shows a pale woman with listless brown hair, ashen cheeks, and an undernourished, unsmiling mouth. Only her startled eyes suggest the energy Wendy imagines murder must require.

"The megachurch Cora went to?" the boy is saying. "It's basically a cult."

"No wonder she offed the preacher," Megan says. "I mean, she goes to this place for peace and comfort, and they just mess her up more."

"They must have been *brutal*. Brutality masquerading as holiness."

It could be Wendy and Fiona talking—if they still talked. She knew the boy must be Fiona's as soon as Megan named the senior she'd met in the high school band. *Harris McAllister.* She pronounced it tenderly, wistfully, as though he were a dream anyone would want to have. And he is, Fiona's boy, seventeen now, a lovely young man, a dream—the first newborn Wendy ever kissed, his warm wrinkled head soft and yeasty, fresh from her best friend's tortured insides. She last knew him as a gleeful two-year-old, smearing chocolate across a dingy duplex wall blocks from Tate Street Coffee where Fiona and Wendy, in their thrift-shop dresses and steel-toed boots, used to study and plot.

Fifteen years Wendy's heard not a word, and then this boy appears at her door, wearing a bright, busy knitted hat with side tassels, a hat that looks like it can't decide whether it's Peruvian or Norwegian or the result of an abandoned attempt to knit an Orthodox Jew out of stoplight-colored yarn. That's the sort of thing Wendy used to say to Fiona to try to make her laugh.

Here came Fiona's quick dark eyes flashing at Wendy once again—the boy grinning at her and Megan through the storm door, September bright and hot behind him, the leaves still clinging to the trees—and she's as weak for that flash as ever she was. How could she not make a feast of the boy? She took his polite extended hand, clasped it a little too warmly, and pulled him by his long spiderish arm over the threshold. She offered seltzer, coffee, cookies, and welcomed him to sit on the sofa next to her daughter to hunt demons or zombies or whatever the fuck it is they go after.

Sophomore year, UNC Greensboro, 1991: Wendy's smoking out front of McIver after Renaissance Poetry when this lanky girl with dyed-black hair borrows her lighter. As cleaner-cut students cross the sun-dappled campus paths, the girl tells Wendy the filthiest joke she's ever heard another girl tell. Delighted, Wendy asks her name. *Fiona*. Delighted again.

The following afternoon, there she is in Intro to Theater—the dirty-joke girl! Wendy liked acting; Fiona, the black-clothed tech jobs. Important things occurred out in the world—the aftermath of the Gulf War, Waco, the Rodney King trial—but what was all that, next to *The Taming of the Shrew* or *The Little Foxes*? Semester after semester, each play was a self-contained world they inhabited intensely for a time, then left behind forever.

They became Wendy and Fiona, a package deal wherever they went. Back then, she'd have told you their kids would grow up as close as siblings. Instead, Megan and Harris are slowly getting acquainted Saturday after Saturday over the noise of their games. Megan made Wendy promise not to spy on them when Harris came over. Wendy's husband, Chris, demanded just as adamantly that she keep an eye on the kids.

"What on earth can they do with the door open and me wandering around the house?"

"You never know," Chris scowled.

"Megan's a good girl, she makes straight A's."

"So did you."

True. Wendy made dean's list the same semester she rode high and shirtless down Battleground Avenue in Fiona's crappy car, scarfing hot Krispy Kreme doughnuts and screaming the words to "Welcome to the Jungle"—ironically, of course—as the wind whipped and mingled their long hair.

She said to Chris, "Dude, after all that mess in middle school, you should be grateful she has a nice friend."

"I'd be *grateful* if he was also a freshman. And a girl."

Quick peek into the den: Megan sits cross-legged against the pillows banked in one corner of the sofa. She watches Harris, who's leaning forward, elbows on knees, gripping the bat-shaped controller. He watches the figure on the screen intently, as though, if he could, he'd eat it, or kiss it, or worse. The figure runs, jumps, shoots, jumps, circles back, pockets treasure, and runs again. As Harris frantically taps buttons, he explains to Megan details about the game's strategy that she's belabored to Wendy many times.

"Oh," Megan says to him, "it's *super* smart you figured that out."

Not a shred of sarcasm. She's *fawning*. Pretending it's all news to her and he's the genius. Ugh. Did Wendy teach her to act like that?

Back in the day, Fiona and Wendy would have had things to say about such a performance.

Pretty soon, Wendy would've said, this girl is going to be sorry.

Oh, *this* girl, Fiona would've answered—sliding a loose fist back and forth near her lips and pretending to gag—pretty soon, *this* girl is going to wind up on her knees.

SOON IT'S A regular thing, Harris and Megan gaming on Saturday afternoons. Whenever he stays for dinner, he wears his silly hat at the table—slight points off for Fiona—but he says *please* and *thank you*, unlike Chris, too busy shoveling food into his mouth to do more than nod. *He eats the same way he fucks,* Wendy told Fiona, before she knew she'd love him, much less marry him. *All hulked over and in a rush, like he's got somewhere he needs to go after.* Then, she took his haste for passion. Now she knows it's mostly appetite.

Harris always responds graciously to Chris's barrage of questions. Talking comes naturally to the boy. He has his mother's gift for putting people at ease. At parties, Fiona lavished attention on everybody she met, asking them all about themselves, enthusing over whatever they said without ever sounding fake. Meantime, Wendy would hook up with any old boy, needing a talkless way to pass the time until Fiona was ready to go.

"I'm working at a pizza place now," Harris said, the first time he stayed for dinner. "But I want to major in graphic design when I go to college. If you don't mind me asking, sir, what do you do?"

Megan gave Wendy the quick, secret smile they share when they're getting the best of her dad and he doesn't have a clue. Wendy wondered if her daughter primed Harris to ask this question. Chris loves explaining the intricacies of his duties as shipping and receiving manager for an easy-chair company.

"Well, basically, I run interference between the sales people, the warehouse staff, and the bossman's incompetent son. Everything's a puzzle, all the time, and it's up to me to solve it. Like today, for instance, I had to figure out why my Lubbocks in Desert Sand went to my Charlotte store instead of here to Greensboro."

Since his promotion to manager, he's all "my." My chairs, my stores, my trucks, my guys.

"So you're like constantly putting out fires," Harris said. "Sounds like a tough job—you must be really organized."

"It's a lot to keep track of, that's for sure."

He began to warm to the boy—after all, Chris likes a pat on the head as much as anyone. Every year at the company holiday party, his gross boss puts his gross arm around Wendy and says he doesn't know what he'd do without her husband. It's Christmas, so she plays nice. She says, "Me, either," and Chris beams. He thinks she's forgotten the first five years of their marriage, when she had to take care of everything—Megan, money, the house, *everything*—because he couldn't stand growing up. Wendy always had a job—sometimes a full-time *and* a part-time—while Chris was always losing jobs because he was too hung over to go to work the morning after a Green Day concert or a night out with his buddies from his failed band. He left the dishes and laundry to pile up, never fixed a meal. He spent money they didn't have and then forgot to pay the bills. He insisted Megan stay in day care because he needed to look for work, then dragged his feet about looking for work.

Wendy laid down an ultimatum. He apologized, he begged, he loved her more than the sun and the moon, *I wrote you a song, baby. Don't go.* The whole bullshit package. More ultimatums, more scenes. She would have left except she was a sucker for contrition. And then: a miracle. When Megan was four, he miraculously got the job at the furniture company, which he even more miraculously turned out to be good at, and—most miraculously of all—actually liked. Wendy stopped having to worry about whether she could depend on him for basic things. Chris stepping up to his responsibilities felt like all the miracle she'd ever need in her marriage. She knew plenty of women who weren't so lucky.

"And what about you?" Harris said that first evening, turning to Wendy. "What do you do?"

"Me? I'm an administrative assistant in a law firm."

"Any chance you're working on the Cora Goodnight case?"

"Oh, brother," said Chris. "Wendy's obsessed with that woman."

"I'd be nervous if I was you, Dad," Megan joked, making a stabby motion with her spoon.

"We do family law, not criminal cases," Wendy said.

"I'm stalking Cora Goodnight," Harris grinned. "Online, I mean."

Wendy understood. That same morning, after reading the latest developments in Cora's case—they'd finally assembled a jury and the evidence was now being heard—she'd Googled Fiona again: two old addresses and a Facebook page with forty-seven friends, set to private. No Twitter or Instagram, no LinkedIn, not even a Goodreads. Wendy had searched her name in the county tax records to see if she owned a home and, if so, where she lived. Nothing. No internet sensation, Fiona McAllister.

"She was *super* devious." Harris paused to lick chili from his hat's golden tassel, then launched into an informed analysis of Cora's lethal combinations of ordinary household cleaners. Megan raised her eyebrows at her mother: *See how smart he is?*

"That woman had a hard life," Chris said, reaching for the bread.

Journalists relished detailing the lifetime of abuse heaped on Cora: drunk mother, hands-on stepfathers, learning disabilities, charlatans paid to miracle-heal her limp. At eighteen, she married a man no better than the other people she'd tried to love. He died prematurely, as did her second husband, and everybody said she had the worst luck. Then she wed a third time, a wounded Persian Gulf veteran who regularly laid his cane across his wife's back to remind her that her weakness exceeded his. Before long, he turned up dead, too, another "accident."

"You kids are lucky. Guys in my warehouse—they've got dads in jail, moms on drugs, poor situation, no opportunity. You have to think about what that does to a person before you judge."

"Who's judging?" Megan protested. "Don't get mad at me! Everybody knows her life was horrible."

Whenever Harris stays for supper, they have to eat in the dining room instead of at the tiny kitchen table. Wendy's never liked this room. At sundown, the yellow walls sour from cheerful butter to wan buttermilk, and once it's fully dark outside, the windows become mean black patches that put them on display to anybody passing by.

"Paint the room a different color." Fiona would have said. "And we'll make some curtains. It's not hard."

Fiona on her best days got shit done. Wendy itches to ask Harris a million questions about her, but she doesn't want Chris figuring out he's Fiona's kid, not yet. Chris used to call Fiona a user—not drugs, people—which was funny to Wendy, because Fiona thought the same of Chris. When either of them said it, Wendy thought, *I guess I have a type.*

So far Harris has mentioned only that his mother sells plants at a nursery, is twice divorced, and named their cat Bogart, which Harris thought for the longest time was a reference to the boggarts in Harry Potter.

"Those dudes Cora killed totally deserved it," Megan says one night when Harris brings pizzas and they're all sitting in the yellow gloom.

"Ah, the moral certainty of untested youth," Wendy says. They all ignore her.

Chris objects that nobody deserves to be murdered.

Harris can't help feeling sorry for Cora, even though he's 100 percent certain she's guilty.

Wendy takes another slice and says nothing. Whenever she reads about Cora's victims, all she can think is, "What did you do, man, to push her that far?"

IN OCTOBER, MEGAN cuts off the hair she's been growing since third grade. New planes and angles emerge in her face. Her Instagram shows moments her mother's not privy to in real life: Megan and Harris standing on the edge of the shopping-center fountain, pointing at funny signs, goofing around. They practice music together on the deck—Megan trombone, Harris trumpet—driving the neighbors' dogs into frenzies of barking. And of course they play their endless bloody games, hour upon hour.

Months used to go by when Wendy didn't think of Fiona at all. But now, eating lunch salad at her desk at Crumpler, Bearden & Applewhite Family Law, or trying to fall asleep at night, she recalls episodes she hasn't thought about in years. At first, each remembered incident is a solitary, gentle tug, but as the weeks pass and the trees grow bare, more memories wash up. By Thanksgiving, they're lapping up one right after the other, bringing a tide that pulls her out into bigger water. She begins to fantasize: first, a revival of their friendship; then a deepening.

Recently her mind keeps returning to the night of the cast party for *As You Like It*. She and Fiona drank rum and Coke and smoked cloves in a ramshackle house where theater and music majors lived.

They danced until their hair dripped with sweat, then wandered into a bedroom. On top of trench coats and peacoats and army-navy surplus jackets, they tested each other's softness with tongues spiced and boozy as a Christmas cake.

The specifics of the encounter have evaporated, mostly. Wendy remembers the scratch of wool under her bare leg as Fiona pulled up her skirt, a sliver of party light changing colors beneath a door, Talking Heads playing on a distant stereo. Touching Fiona / Fiona touching her felt deeply familiar and also unfamiliar...Fiona's breasts were more compact than Wendy's, her pubic hair finer. Wendy had never predicted she might shyly slide her fingers inside another woman (much less Fiona). Nor had she imagined how welcome it might be to encounter smooth, cool hands that didn't try to knead and poke her into submission.

Fiona didn't bother with incredulity. She did not hesitate, she did not rush. After a few minutes, neither did Wendy.

Where did they go after the party? Where did they sleep? What did they say? All Wendy knows is, they never talked about what happened, not seriously. If one of them alluded to it, the other made a joke, subject closed. They shelved their encounter with all the ridiculous, fun, wonderful, irresponsible, dangerous things they did so many other nights when drunk or high or simply young.

For years Wendy told herself, when she remembered to think about it, that what happened that night was just a youthful experiment, meaningless. But now she's convinced it must mean something, the fact that she still remembers that—*that*—as she sits eating the ten-thousandth salad of her life under the fluorescent lights of

Crumpler, Bearden & Applewhite. What she remembers is a mutual, tender confusion, edged with possibility. Then somebody threw open the door, looking for their coat, and the potential vanished like smoke. For so long she thought nothing had changed after, but now, as she eats salad 10,001, salad 10,002, salad 10,003, it dawns on her that there was a shift. Before that night, they functioned as different but equal partners in the friendship. Afterward, it seems to Wendy now, Fiona grew more confident, more vivid and appealing, while Wendy became paler, less distinct, slightly—how to put it?—*reduced.*

She'd known something was off but not how to fix it. Still, she continued eagerly following her friend's brightness wherever it chose to go.

AT THE BAND'S HOLIDAY concert in December, Wendy spies on the other side of the auditorium a woman she's sure is Fiona. She's tall, with dark hair, and slouches exactly how Fiona used to, her boots up on the back of the wooden seat in front of her. Chris doesn't ask Wendy what she's looking at. He's too busy fiddling with his phone camera, getting it ready to video the performance. The woman Wendy's watching sits with her head tilted back, staring up at the ceiling. She doesn't talk to anyone around her, not once, which is unlike the Fiona Wendy loved but very like the Fiona she stopped talking to. Never once the whole evening does the woman look in her direction, even though Wendy wills her to turn her head, the way she used to try to move stuff with her mind when she was ten years old.

After the concert, they wait for Megan in the packed lobby. It's impossible to find Fiona amid the sea of people bundling themselves up to brave the cold night, but as soon as Wendy sees Harris's garish hat bobbing through the crowd, she makes a beeline. He's standing with a blond woman, a man in a dark suit, and two little girls in velvet dresses and Mary Janes.

"Wendy?" the man says.

His name comes back like a bad penny.

"Hi, Reece."

Harris's father wears gold cufflinks and has a thick, expensive overcoat folded over his arm. He might be Crumpler or Bearden; his sculpted, painted wife could be Applewhite. She greets Wendy politely, without interest. When Reece mentions Wendy's association with Fiona, his wife hurries the girls off to the ladies' room.

"Wait, you know my mom?" Harris says to Wendy, just as Chris and Megan break through the crowd to join them.

She pretends she's never connected the dots before now. What a coincidence! Her acting training comes right back.

"Is she here?" She looks around at the dwindling crowd.

"She couldn't make it," Harris says.

Reece does a thing with his face that obviously means *typical Fiona,* which makes Wendy hate him extra.

In the car Chris carries on about how he knew something was shady about that boy, Megan defends Harris, and Wendy insists she had no clue he was Fiona's kid.

"It's Reece you ought to dislike," she tells Chris. "The way he left Fiona high and dry when Harris was only six months old."

After Reece left, Fiona clawed at the confines of single motherhood, desperate to open any hole that might let her breathe. Wendy moved in with her and kept the baby in the evenings so Fiona could wait tables. Occasionally, she didn't return until the next morning, bearing donuts and tales of shenanigans Wendy thought they were getting a little old for. She liked it better when they fell asleep in her bed watching television, the baby bundled between them. Next morning, he'd wake happy, his smiles and babble cut from the same cloth as the sunrise and the birdsong.

In the evenings, when Wendy came home from her office job— she'd been saving to go to graduate school to become a dramaturge, money she'd later spend on day care—she'd take Harris to the park so Fiona could shower and dress for work. Sometimes she bought him a Cadbury egg, a special treat. However delicately he bit, the egg always smushed in his hands, and they laughed when the sugary goo ran out—each collapse a familiar but still funny punchline—while Fiona dampened a paper towel to clean up the mess.

Sometimes Fiona got so fed up caring for Harris that Wendy could've sworn she hated him. How could you hate your own baby? Wendy didn't understand Fiona's anger because she wasn't really a mother yet. She was only pretending. Nor did she know what to feel when, other days, Fiona's love for her son left no room for Wendy.

But they did okay. Harris was well cared for. Those two years may not have felt like an especially good time when they were living them, but now Wendy remembers that spell as a kind of honeymoon.

Then Reece remarried. Fiona crashed. Stopped going out, stopped opening the curtains. She ate only kid food: mac and cheese, goldfish crackers, the grapes Wendy cut in half. Her lost, looping talk chased her ex-husband round and round. She loved him madly; she hated him madly. Whenever Reece took Harris for his allotted time, she got migraines—blindness, vomiting, the works. He'd married again only to punish her, he didn't care about their child, he wanted to steal her child, he thought this new woman would be a better mother.

"I don't think he and the deuce are actually all that interested in Harris," Wendy said. "She probably wants her own baby anyway. Look, you freaked out about Y2K, too, about the computers losing their minds and the power grid shutting down, and that didn't happen. It's going to be okay."

But worry dogged Fiona. Misery leaked from her like sap from a tree until she was sticky with it. It was like living with Chicken Little, the hopeless sky forever looming closer. Wendy moved in with Chris. He was so much easier. Finally, when Fiona kept refusing to see a doctor for either the headaches or her depression, Wendy took oxycodone from her mother's medicine cabinet and left the bottle on Fiona's kitchen counter. The next time she dropped by, she handed Harris his egg and asked her friend if the oxy was helping her headaches.

"I'm not taking that shit. It's addictive. I gave them to Jerry to sell."

"Selling them on the street is illegal."

"So is stealing them," Fiona said, in the flat, dead tone Wendy dreaded, the same one in which she droned to Harris minutes later—chocolate on the apartment wall, on his clothes—"Honey, don't do that."

Talking to Fiona had become like spitting into the wind. How could you help a person who wouldn't help herself? For a few days, Wendy didn't call or go by, telling herself she just needed a little break, a breathing space. Their lives had been entwined so long she didn't know how to pick them looser without tearing something crucial. The few days turned into a week, then two, and Fiona never called, not once. It hurt Wendy not to be needed or missed. The two weeks turned into three, four. The weeks turned into months.

Wendy mentioned the rift to her mother, omitting the pills, which her mother assumed she'd misplaced.

"Well, I never trusted that girl," her mother said, before repeating her "two cents" about how exclusive friendships were unhealthy. Wendy regretted confiding in her. Her mother was a lonely woman who still removed an earring to talk on the telephone. She had few women friends and had never been able to grasp exactly what men wanted from her. Bosses, plumbers, salesmen—all were baffling. She had no clue how to repel the neighbors who came around when she was between husbands, wanting to advise her about car repair and lawn upkeep and the mailbox that kept falling over because the hole the post was buried in was too wide and forgiving.

"This is the best time of your life," she said wistfully over her rosé. "You're young, you have a nice man. You shouldn't limit yourself."

Wendy nodded, certain that her mother, as usual, had no idea what she was talking about.

WENDY IS BEGINNING to accept that she'll never reconnect with Fiona when the judge declares a mistrial due to faulty handling of evidence, and Cora Goodnight is released. The same week—an unseasonably warm week for February—Chris finally agrees to let Megan, now fifteen, go out with Harris in his car for the first time.

"As long as they come home right after the movie. Home by 9:30. Ten at the latest."

Chris makes Harris give him his number before they leave, and Wendy can tell Megan wants to kill her father. When the kids finally ride off in Harris's beat-up Toyota Corolla, Wendy opens beers. Chris grills burgers while she tosses a salad. The house is weirdly quiet without their daughter's pulsing, thumping music, and it pains Wendy to know she'll have to get used to that, when Megan goes for good.

The sun sets, but it's still not that cold. They put on their coats and eat off plastic plates by the backyard fire pit, talking about vacations they'd take if they had more money. Chris wants to see Yosemite. Wendy votes for Seattle, where she and Fiona yearned to go, back in the heyday of grunge. Chris says the new guy in the warehouse is turning out worse than useless. Wendy tells him Applewhite offered to pay for her to take a paralegal course.

"I was thinking it would be good to have a new thing to engage my mind, now that Megan doesn't need me at home as much."

"Mind, hell," he says, "paralegal would be a good promotion. We could use the scratch."

Mind, hell. For a minute Wendy doesn't like him again, but then he hands her another beer and asks if she's warm enough.

At 9:15, he starts checking his phone and pacing over to the driveway to see if the kids have returned. At ten, he says, "I never should have let you talk me into this."

"They just lost track of time, Chris. I'll text them."

"Tell the kid he's going to be wearing his dick for a necktie if he doesn't get my daughter home thirty minutes ago."

"Oh, Chris, listen to yourself. Maybe they had car trouble. That car's really old."

"Shit!" He holds up his phone. "She's turned off her location so I can't see where they are! That can't be good. I'm just going to go look for them—that's what I'm going to do."

"Do you even know which movie theater they went to?"

"By now, they're not *at* a theater, Wendy. Duh. How dumb can you be?"

He jabs the fire, stirring up a spray of orange sparks. A few drift over to her jeans, and one by one she extinguishes them with the beer bottle's wet bottom: Megan helping Harris unhook her bra; her breasts shy and eager in his tricky hands; his mouth on her warm neck that has smelled since babyhood of oatmeal soap and lavender laundry detergent; his fingers under the waistband of the fifth pair of jeans she tried on this afternoon . . .

"Let me call her," Wendy says.

Voicemail.

Chris jingles his keys. "You sit tight. In case they come back."

"They're good kids," she calls, but he's gone.

Sit tight. The phrase strikes her as vaguely funny, given that she's sitting and she *is* tight after three beers. Overhead the stars blink as though fighting to come on all the way. Sit tight. Hang tight. Cora Goodnight won't hang tight. She's been released. She's free. No death penalty for her. Wendy giggles, then chides herself: not funny. Besides, they don't hang people anymore, do they? Is it electric chair still or lethal injection? Gas chamber? Barbarity. Executioner. What a job. Murder should be personal. You should only kill someone because you're certain in your heart of hearts they need to be dead, immediately, and no one and nothing else is going to get them dead fast enough . . .

. . . Megan wincing as Harris enters her . . .

Oh, look, Wendy's drinking another beer. Well, why not, if it helps her worry less.

. . . Megan turning her head toward the stale back seat, scared that this weird intrusion is all her dreams will amount to . . .

Wait. Maybe beer makes her worry more? Not less? Maybe she's on the wrong track. Has Harris even returned Megan's flirting? Wendy's not sure she understands what constitutes flirting between kids these days. She knows boys harass girls to send naked pictures on their phones. Or that girls offer them, unasked. She doesn't think Megan would be dumb enough . . . but then again. Wendy knows what it is to want so much to please someone. Impossible now to count the long-ago mouths, the hands—in bathrooms and under bushes, on sofas and beds and beer-sticky floors—the hands and tongues she invited, opened herself to, praying they'd kiss and lick and stroke away all her wanting. All the while wondering what Fiona was doing . . . Later, when she recounted the sloppy details, hoping to make Fiona jealous, Fiona just shrugged and said it hadn't been much of a party, and Wendy wondered why they'd bothered to go at all.

Then that one party, after which everything changed but they pretended it didn't.

Faulty handling. Good for Cora, getting off on a mistrial. Wendy imagines the day Travis Goodnight fell. She pictures the roadside mountain overlook, Cora relishing the silence after his holler dwindles, then ceases, and she can finally breathe the still open air, the miles of treetops a green balm to her eyes, the hawks wheeling free in the

oh, shit, here he comes . . . Travis Goodnight . . . back from the dead.

No, that's crazy.

But somebody is walking through the gate and across the backyard. Somebody tall. Chris? Harris? No. The stride is different.

A wiry woman in a peacoat, walking with her head up like a long-legged animal that gets its information from the air.

"Fiona!"

Wendy stands too fast. A dizzy, molten heat flows across her chest and shoots up into her face. She's played this reunion in her head a thousand times but never figured out how to make it go smoothly.

"Wendy." Fiona keeps her hands in her pockets. There's to be no hug, evidently.

"Want a beer?"

"I don't drink anymore."

"Oh," Wendy says. "Well, that's probably a good idea."

"Why's that?"

"For anybody, I mean," she hurries to say. "Giving it up. Stopping. At our age. I mean, I should probably quit drinking myself. Then I wouldn't babble incoherent shit when an old friend suddenly drops by."

"Yes, you would," Fiona says. She nearly smiles. Or maybe it's just a play of the firelight across her face that makes Wendy think so.

"Look," Fiona goes on, "your husband threatened Harris. Our phones are set up where I can see his texts."

She held out her phone: "UR gonna regret keeping my kid out 2 late, you little shit."

"Harris lets you do that? See his texts?"

"He doesn't have a choice these days, not after some of the shit he's pulled. He's been in a little trouble, nothing serious, but Reece insists . . . Look, can we just focus on the problem with your husband right now? I see *he* hasn't changed much."

"Chris just gets really worked up when he's worried. It's Megan's first time out in a car with a boy, and Harris was supposed to have Megan—."

"Who threatens a kid, though? Who does that?"

"Well, Harris *was* supposed to have Megan home by now."

"Harris is a *kid*."

A kid the size of a large man, Wendy thinks. Her phone bleats. Urgent texts from Megan, one after another, like storm warnings.

Stranded at park by science center

near pond with paddleboats

dumb H lost keys. Went to look. Not answering text.

I'm alone.

It dark.

Scared.

"They're stranded at the science center. But I've had too many beers to drive," Wendy says.

"Gimme the keys to your car."

"Wait, how'd you get here?"

"Lyft. We only have the one car, Wendy. My ship never came in, if you've been wondering."

Wendy hands over the keys to her Prius. Neighborhood to neighborhood, a few lingering Christmas lights breach the darkness. By the time they pass the Krispy Kreme on Battleground Avenue, the silence is awful.

"Remember when we used to—"

"I'm not doing that memory lane shit with you, Wendy. We're just making sure the kids are safe. That's all this is."

Fiona stares at the road ahead, her profile insistently passive against the scrolling backdrop of closed stores and late-night restaurants.

"Okay. Well, did you see that Cora Goodnight got off? Harris says y'all have been following the case. I'm kind of glad. I didn't really want her to go to jail."

"Why not? She murdered people. She's fucking terrifying. Why would you not want somebody like that to go to jail?"

"I don't know," Wendy says. Fiona's vehemence surprises her. "I guess . . . it just seems like she had such a hard life, and all her victims were so horrible to her."

"Plenty of people get treated badly but they don't *murder* anybody."

Wendy waits a few minutes in silence, then says, "I can't believe you're still so mad at me. After all this time."

Nothing.

"You could have called me, too, you know. If you really wanted me around."

"Oh, for fuck's sake!"

Fiona brakes hard and the seatbelt cuts into Wendy's chest. The stoplight's glare reddens Fiona's cheek as she turns toward Wendy. Her lips are thinner than they used to be, her mouth tougher. The half-inch scar on her chin looks old but is new to Wendy.

"That is just like you," Fiona says. "You always had to be blameless, so you blamed everybody else."

"I tried to help you, but whatever I did was never enough."

"You were basically my son's other *parent*, Wendy, and you fucking *ghosted*."

There's no denying that. The light changes. Fiona steps on the gas, and they hurtle forward.

"You know what happened after you left that shit at my house? Those fucking pills? I looked at the bottle for hours. Then I took one pill and put it on my tongue. I wanted to see what my death was going to taste like. Sounds dramatic, huh? But that's exactly what I was doing. That's where my head was at back then. And *you knew it*."

They're speeding too fast for comfort, lights and signs rushing by. Wendy feels sick.

"You said you gave them to what's-his-face. To sell," she says. "So you could buy groceries."

"Well, I lied. You want to know what actually happened? What actually happened was, I mashed all the pills up and put them in a glass of Jack and Coke. And I stared at that for a while. And then Harris started crying from his bed and I poured that shit down the toilet."

They pass the park gate. Fiona makes a vicious U-turn and pulls the Prius up behind the empty Corolla. They get out and hurry past the locked gate and its warning not to trespass on city property after sundown. Under the clouded night sky, they can barely see the park road through the woods. Wendy turns her phone toward the pavement to light it.

"You might as well have put a gun in my hand," Fiona says.

"It wasn't what I meant," Wendy starts. But what had she meant?

They follow the light jerking along the road, Fiona's hands jammed in her pockets, Wendy breathing fast, trying to keep up.

"You could never just let me be," Fiona says. "You couldn't just let me be sad when Reece left."

"He was horrible."

"He *was* horrible," she agrees. "He's still horrible, actually."

Wendy hears the slightest give in Fiona's voice, a tiny relenting, and suddenly the old want bristles all through her. It grows as they walk on together through the dark wood, it increases until the trees and the air are pregnant with it. Even the dirt under their feet is fat with her wanting, that force she's never figured out how to reckon with, as though it were some ancient pagan spirit too large and unknowable to be appeased.

"He was horrible, but I was sad anyway," Fiona says.

"I know."

"And you couldn't just let me have it, my sadness. Because it wasn't about you."

"No."

The road has led them to the pond. The low lights dotting its perimeter reflect as white smudges in the water. Toward the middle, the pond's glassy surface voids into blackness. They pass swings and slides, walking toward the picnic area, where Wendy used to bring

Megan and before that, but only once, Harris. The goats at the petting zoo scared him. He cried and refused his lunch. At home afterward, she read to him before his nap, and he pointed to a fox stealing
an egg from a henhouse.

"That's you," he said. "Bringing my egg."

Megan sits on a picnic table, her phone a footlight for her tragic
face. *Safe, safe,* is all Wendy can think.

As they walk back to the cars, Megan confesses that instead of going to a movie after dinner, they drove to Cora Goodnight's house.
They recognized it from the news: a dumpy aluminum-sided ranch,
painted sour-apple green, with a wreath of fake white flowers on the
door. A normal, boring house—not murder-y enough, a disappointment. Wendy's driven by it herself. She's driven by Cora's church, too,
a cavernous metal building next to a carpet outlet. But its plain fa-
cade told her nothing about what must have occurred there to blast
the last sediments of hope from Cora's face and bare the bedrock of
fear that was her only dependable truth.

The first year of their estrangement, Wendy rode by Fiona's duplex nearly every week. She was dying to talk to the old, fun Fiona
who, when she chose to, made Wendy feel like she was the only person Fiona cared about. But Wendy was scared *that* Fiona was gone
forever, so she never stopped to share the news of her quick courthouse wedding or Megan's birth. A few times she spied Harris in the
yard, playing with an older neighbor child. She longed to show him
the baby screaming in the back seat, furious at having for a mother a
voyeur who never stopped to see what she'd come to see.

The two police cars parked on Cora's street made Harris nervous, so the kids didn't stick around. Megan won't say what happened when they got to the park, and Wendy won't press her in front of Fiona. Back at the gate, Harris is lying on the hood of the Corolla, face turned up to the sky.

Fiona shouts, "Find the keys?"

"Affirmative," he says, in a robot voice. And then, "Stars are the whitest white in the white-a-verse."

"Oh, shit," Fiona sighs. She pulls him up to sitting. He's laughing as she does it; he doesn't care if he's in trouble. She sniffs his jacket, then yanks off his hat and smells that, too.

He puts his hands up in the air and says, "We didn't smoke. Swear to God."

"You don't believe in God!" Fiona backhands his shoulder once, then a second time, harder.

"But He believes in me," Harris says in a singsong and laughs some more.

Wendy leans to smell Megan's hair. Wow. How did she miss the skunk when they hugged earlier? She's surprised. She thought kids didn't smoke real weed anymore. Bona fide naturalists, these two.

Megan moans, "Dad's going to kill me."

"He's not going to kill you," Wendy says. "But obviously there will be consequences."

"*Obviously,*" says Fiona. "Come on, everybody, get in the car. I'll drive you home so you can work out the *consequences.*"

"Don't you think they should be punished?"

Fiona stares out into the woods for a minute, making a show of choosing *not* to say what she wants to say. Then she turns to Harris.

"Give me the bag."

"What?"

"The weed. Give it here."

Harris digs around in his clothes and brings out a small plastic baggie. Fiona takes it, grabs Wendy's arm with her left hand, and jams her right roughly into Wendy's jeans pocket, straining the fabric as she shoves the bag in as far as the pocket allows. Her face nearly touches Wendy's as she leans in and says, "There you go, Miss Consequences."

She backs off, then says, "I have to go to work in the morning, so we're all taking my car. Mr. Tough Guy can bring you to get yours tomorrow, Wendy."

She throws herself into the driver's side of the Corolla and slams the door. Wendy's head thuds, the beers taking their toll. The old want has fled; the old disappointment is back, along with a terrible thirst. She walks over to the trash can at the head of the path and drops the bag inside.

"Aw, man," the boy moans. "What a fucking waste."

BACK HOME, MEGAN immediately runs upstairs to shower. Chris is washing dishes.

"You left the fire burning," he scolds. "In the backyard. Lucky the whole neighborhood didn't go up in flames."

"What were you going to do, Chris? If you found the kids? Beat Harris up?"

He scrubs furiously, not looking at her. She downs a glass of water, then another. The kitchen light is harsh. Her head pounds. Tomorrow, she'll feel like garbage when Chris drives her to the park to pick up her car. Tomorrow, she'll have to decide whether to tell him the whole story. *They were actually smoking real weed*, she imagines telling him, *not vaping some weird pot juice. You'd think it was cool if it wasn't your kid.*

After a minute he says, sheepish, "Is she okay?"

"Mostly. I'll go check on her."

Upstairs, Megan is studying the old glow-in-the-dark stars stuck on her ceiling. Wendy turns down the music and sits beside her on the bed. Megan swears it was her first time. She didn't even do it right, she thinks, because she doesn't feel high, just stupid.

"I told him I *like* liked him. So stupid. He actually *laughed*. He basically thinks I'm an *infant*. It doesn't help that you and Dad treat me like such a baby."

"Well, there *is* a big difference between a senior and a freshman."

"And you! The way you've been acting this whole time, all super friendly to him. It's so weird. It's like you *wanted* him to have a crush on you."

Earlier, as Wendy and Megan got out of the Corolla, Harris said, "I hope we can still be friends." She'd thought he was talking to Megan, but maybe that remark had been for her?

"Honey, that's ridiculous. Harris doesn't have a crush on me. I'm just an old lady to him. And if it seemed like I was being extra nice, it's only because I have a soft spot for him. I mean, I was there when he was born. *Before* he was born. He was like...I don't know."

She almost said "like my child," but she can't say that because Megan *is* her child and hates competition. And anyway, it doesn't matter what Harris meant, because nobody is remaining friends. After he spoke, Fiona put her forehead down on the steering wheel, and when Wendy thanked her for the ride, she threw up a hand: *Sure, whatever, go.*

Oblivious that something in her mother has crumpled, Megan keeps haranguing her.

"Honestly? You want my honest opinion? You're so desperate for people to like you. You're like a total ass-kisser who just begs for attention from *literally* anybody, even if it hurts your own daughter."

Maybe she has a point. Maybe Wendy has always been so hungry for attention that she'll take any kind. Why else would she sit here and let Megan try to humiliate her, unless she thinks abuse is better than nothing?

Chris opens the door, sees their faces, and quickly shuts it again.

They laugh.

"He's afraid we're going to cry," Wendy says.

"Tears are man repellent," Megan says. "They can't handle it. At the park? After Harris said he wasn't interested in me romantically? He was all like, oh, no, don't cry! don't cry! And I was like, well, then don't give me something to cry about!"

"Oh, honey."

Wendy lies down and works her arm under Megan's shoulders. The girl snuggles up. After a few minutes she says she wishes she could take back what she said.

"Forget it," Wendy says. "We're okay. Nothing could make us not be okay."

IN THE DEN LATER, she turns on her favorite prison drama. Chris sits out back drinking one last beer beside the banked fire. Next, he'll take out the trash and lock the doors, then come find Wendy. He won't apologize for being hotheaded. She won't admit maybe she was a little blind about Harris. In bed, Chris'll either drop right to sleep or pull her toward him; she seldom has to wait to learn how things will go with him.

On the television, one orange-clad woman hides her face between the naked thighs of another. Wendy hopes nobody barges in to ruin their good time. She knows better than to believe TV shows, but she can't help liking when they claim it's always possible to find love—even in prison, between the turf wars and shivvings and rapes, even if only for a moment. Wouldn't it be ironic if Cora Goodnight, by evading conviction, missed her chance at love?

But what does Wendy know of prisons, really? She's only ever driven past them. Each summer of her girlhood, she and her mother spent an afternoon in Raleigh at the art museum, next to which stood a glum compound of brick buildings, sharply fenced. Wendy believed this was the state penitentiary, and to stop herself thinking about the horrors of the electric chair, she imagined the doomed men as spirits, free to wander, immune to the barbs of concertina wire. No longer dead men walking, they were not executed, but escaped. Flown.

Eventually she learned the facility was a youth prison—no electric chair. The fences and buildings are long gone, yet whenever she visits the museum with Megan, she still fancies her flown men shadowing her in the museum's dim, carpeted galleries. Together they gaze on the antique beauty of Audubon's mammoth folios, his stunning birds. Painted with such cruel precision, not from life, as she used to believe, but postmortem: killed purposely to make it easier for the artist to render them. *What did you do to wind up here?* she'd wanted to ask the flown, back when she was a girl. Now that she's grown, the question seems rude, and anyway, she figures, they'd probably only shrug and repeat the question back to her.

Delta Foxtrot

One Thursday in October, I went to the restored theater downtown for the film-society showing of *The Thin Man*. Just as the movie started, a handsome man sat two rows in front of me. First I noticed the hair—thick and wavy like my husband's when we first met. Then I found myself studying his profile, how his expression changed as the black-and-white movie menaced us with its long shadows, its echoing footsteps and tilted fedoras. I thought how like a scene in a movie it was: him unaware that I was watching him as he watched the screen, his face alternately illuminated and shadowed by what was playing out above us.

Afterward, the society president announced that we were all welcome to meet for drinks at a restaurant down the street. I'd never gone along before and didn't know anybody in the group, but the hair guy was walking over, so I thought what the hell, why not try to meet some people? Everyone clustered around the bar, waiting to order, and I worked my way through until I stood next to him. He was squinting up at the chalkboard above the bar as if he couldn't quite make out the list of wines and beers.

"How could you see the movie if you can't see that?" I asked.

Though his eyes were small and his nose a bit too thin and sharp, the hair was so luxurious that when he smiled, I felt foolishly pleased with myself.

"I can see what it says," he said, putting out his hand for me to shake. "I just can't decide what I want."

His name was Preston.

"Preston, huh? Like the writer of *The Great McGinty* and *The Palm Beach Story*?" Movies my husband showed me years ago, back when the only dates we could afford were nights at home with a six-pack and a video.

He made a cute little half bow. "I wish I could say that Sturges is my middle name, but it's really Edward."

"The official middle name of the male WASP."

"I had a Jewish grandfather, so I'm not technically a WASP."

"Saved by the mohel!"

He laughed, and I thought, this guy likes to play. When our turn came at the bar, he asked if I'd share a bottle with him. I said I preferred red. The film society people were talking around a big table on the other side of the room, but when the bartender set the Sangiovese and two glasses in front of us, Preston carried them to a small table by the big plateglass windows overlooking the street.

As he poured, he said he was working on a PhD in film studies.

"You seem remarkably cheerful for somebody in that line."

He laughed in a good-natured way; maybe he'd heard that before. "And what do you do?"

"For the last eight years, I've mostly been home with my two children, but now my youngest is in kindergarten. So I work part-time in a paper store." (For some reason, I forgot to say it was my husband's store.) "You know, writing paper, printed invitations, party supplies, that kind of thing."

"You're a *stationer*. That's so wonderfully old-fashioned." He leaned his elbows on the table and gazed at me as he listened. I knew it was partly the wine, partly his determined interest, but I couldn't help looking at that hair and wishing I could get my hands all in it. That he was younger—in his early thirties as opposed to my just turned forty—made his attention all the more flattering.

Each Thursday after that, the film society people sat at their big table, and Preston and I shared a bottle at our two-top. After a few weeks, I realized that he assumed I was separated from my husband. I knew I ought to correct his false impression, but I didn't want him to think I'd assume a man wants to date me just because we shared a few bottles of wine and some laughs.

Each Thursday, I arrived home later—eleven, eleven-thirty, midnight—giddy from flirting, gobbling breath mints, and swearing I would never drive myself again after that many drinks. The house was always quiet when I came in. Even the dog couldn't be bothered to get off his bed and greet me. Upstairs, the bedside lamps would be on, my husband under the covers—a book fallen on his chest, his head lolling to the side—completely unconcerned about my safety or my fidelity.

ON SATURDAYS, MY HUSBAND stayed with the children while I ran errands and visited my father. When Daddy first moved into assisted living, he would scold me.

"You don't have to check on me all the time. Live your life, out

there in the *world*." As though it were a place he was glad to have escaped rather than one he'd fought leaving. But if I didn't come for a
few days, he'd go down to the nurses' station and make them call me.
"Where the hell have you been?" he'd ask when they handed him the
phone. "Down with the clap?"

"Yeah, Daddy. The fleet was in last weekend, and now I'm on
penicillin."

"Serves you right."

My mother would have said that somebody ought to have in-
carcerated my father long ago, but she hadn't lived long enough to
gloat. Four years ago, she'd left her vacation house at Sea Island,
Georgia, put her car key in the ignition, and collapsed on the steering wheel before she could turn it. An aneurysm. Her husband, a retired banker, found her when he came home for lunch after golfing
all morning. "Never knew what hit her," he said when he called, as
if her lack of self-awareness might, for once, make me feel better.
The banker, she'd always maintained, was an afterthought and not
the cause of her split from my father. She and my father had oppos-
ing dispositions—his dark and cynical, hers relentlessly, almost abu-
sively sunny. His rude salty talk was just one of many things about
him that she didn't care for.

"Jesus, Charlie," she'd say, "you cuss like a sailor."

"I *am* a sailor," he'd roar, jostling the ice cubes in his glass to let her
know he needed more scotch.

Sailing was how they'd met, through friends of friends, at a beach
club near Wrightsville in 1964. She'd just graduated from the women's
college; he was forty-two, divorced, a partner at a respected Raleigh

law firm. When they were introduced, he frowned and said, "Well, you're an attractive little thing," as though attractiveness was an obstacle he was going to have to work around.

They were married the next summer. She had double-majored in classics and art history, planning to become a curator, but my father was old-fashioned and didn't want his wife to work. She filled her time volunteering until, after two miscarriages, I came along. I was too late; they were already irreconcilably unhappy, often arguing and worried about money. Sailing remained the one thing they could stand to do together, momentarily forgetting their quarrels as they jibbed and tacked.

They sent me to sailing camp, where I failed to progress. As much as I loved the wind on my face on a sunny day, I couldn't be bothered with navigation and ropes and all the figuring out that the work of sailing required. Even so, nautical terms were our family lingua franca, and it was a regular thing for the three of us to speak as code the names of the flags sailors use to signal other vessels, one flag for each letter of the alphabet. Many an evening my father would come home from the office, glowering, and head straight for the wet bar. If my mother asked him what was the matter, he'd throw up his hand and say "Delta," meaning, *Keep clear of me. I am maneuvering with difficulty.*

I used to try them with my husband, but he'd just raise his eyebrow and say, "Really? A flag? That's all I get?" Even my jokes about semaphornication, complete with hand gestures, couldn't win him over to the flag system.

It was just as well. Married twelve years and together for sixteen, we've developed our own private language. For instance, if he mentions the Civic hatchback he drove when I first knew him, I'll say, *My, she was yar*, and he knows I mean that those were happy days. It's Katharine Hepburn's line in *The Philadelphia Story* about the sailboat Cary Grant designed for their honeymoon. They're divorced, but as soon as she says, *My, she was yar*, with that wistful expression on her face, you know they're going to get back together.

By the time my father went to assisted living, he'd forgotten about the divorce and the banker. When I visited, he would fuss because my mother wasn't there to receive me. "Out shopping," he'd grouse, as though she, not he, had been the impulsive spender. I didn't argue. He'd go on complaining about her, the irritation in his voice so fresh that sometimes I almost believed they were still married, that she was still alive.

The Saturday after Thanksgiving was the first time my children saw my father after he moved into the nursing wing. Assisted living had been bright and lively, with Bingo games and a resident golden retriever. But the nursing wing was "one of those places," as in, when your friends—whose parents are still playing golf and cruising to Puerta Vallarta—say, I'd never put my folks in "one of those places." (To which I say, Good luck with that.) The fluorescent light pressed down on you, the beige walls pressed in on you, and if that wasn't enough to choke you and make you want to run, there were the sick-bed odors, masked by something cloying and purportedly floral. Every now and then the ambulatory patients set off the exit alarm with their ankle bracelets.

The oldest resident, Mrs. Beamon, 101, always parked her wheelchair where you would be forced to walk close to her. Everything about Mrs. Beamon—white hair, ecru bathrobe, pallid skin—was devoid of color except her pink slippers and her baby doll, wrapped in a blue crocheted blanket. This time, when she saw my children, she extended a trembling hand toward them and made a guttural noise.

"Say hello," I prompted Jacob, who was staring at Mrs. Beamon like she was a rare albino animal exhibited behind glass. When he spoke, she gurgled again, and Elsie put her face in my skirt until I told Jacob it was okay to move along.

Down the hall in Room 132, my father's favorite CNA, Bobby, was helping him brush his teeth.

"He's the only one I'll let bathe me," Daddy would say. "He's not queer like most of these male orderlies. He's got seven children and four grandchildren."

"Homosexuals have children, Daddy," I sighed.

"Not in Jamaica, they don't!"

Now my father stared at the television as Bobby handed him a cup of water and held a pink kidney-shaped tray under his mouth. Elsie made a sound of intrigued disgust when Daddy spat, and Jacob nudged her. They started poking and scrapping until I threw them a look.

"Knock-knock," I sang, hating my own false cheer as I rapped on the open door.

Daddy's eyes darted to me, shrunken and angry behind his bifocals. "Foxtrot," he said. The flag that means *I am disabled; communicate with me.*

"It's all right, Mr. Charlie, we're done." Bobby wiped Daddy's chin with a washcloth and stepped back. "Now you're all fresh for a visit with your daughter and your beautiful grandchildren." Bobby was good like that—he always found a subtle way to remind Daddy who I was.

An anguished cry came from across the hall—a man, pleading, "Help me, Father."

Daddy shook his head. "Calling for his priest. Does it all day and night. He can't help it. Poor old bastard doesn't know where he is."

"Yes, it's true," Bobby agreed. "He's confused." With his usual inconspicuous efficiency, he finished straightening the things on the hospital table, then beckoned to the children. "Here's the little man, not so little, what you, about nine?"

"Eight," Jacob said.

"And, Miss Lady, your mama tells me you're a dancer. Is that true?" Elsie shuffle-ball-changed, bit her lip, then added some jazz hands.

"Look at you, with your razzle-dazzle! You see that, Mr. Charlie? Your grandbaby can dance."

Daddy frowned at us, then turned his eyes back toward the television. "Your mother didn't tell me you were coming. She never tells me anything."

BY THE MIDDLE of December, they had put Daddy on oxygen, and I was stopping by the home every day, always missing the doctor on his rounds, never able to find the right nurse who could tell me about my father's condition. With Christmas coming, things were crazy at the store, and the children were hot with Santa fever. Still, I managed to get to film club on Thursday nights. My life at home felt like low-budget mumblecore—a plotless ramble, all awkward pauses and tense situations—and I was looking to Preston to put me in a zippier feature. I yearned for sparkling dialogue, zany capers, dance numbers, and satin gowns cut on the bias. I wanted to drink my morning coffee while wearing a feather-trimmed dressing gown, winking at a man with brilliantined hair on a goddamned train.

Sure enough, one Thursday night Preston walked me to my car, took me in his arms, and kissed me in a way that let me know he'd been wanting to do it for a long time. His lips felt and tasted surprising, different, *wrong*. But also appreciative, eager, and, if not right, then *right on*. We were only kissing, after all. I figured I could stop after kissing and still be considered a faithful wife. When he ran his hand inside my blouse, it was startling but not unwelcome.

Romeo: The way is off my ship. You may feel your way past me.

Soon, though, we had climbed into the back of my Honda—only because it was cold, I reasoned, and we couldn't very well stand around making out in a parking deck, where we might be seen. The car was the perfect spot in which to explain to him that we had to cease at once. But maybe, first, just a *little* more kissing, because that damage was done already, and I might as well enjoy it before I shut it down forever. But then, somehow, pants were off, and it was only a matter of minutes before even I couldn't trick myself, in any way, into thinking I was still a faithful wife.

Alpha: diver below.

Bracing my left foot on the back of the driver's headrest, I abandoned myself to him, not caring that the sharp corner of a juice box was pressing into my behind.

Bravo: I am taking on or discharging explosives.

"I want to be with you," he whispered.

Something in me summoned the wit to say, "Well, of course, you do, after that."

"Come home with me."

I said I'd come to his place on Saturday. I figured I could visit Preston, shower at his place, pick up the dry cleaning, see Daddy, do the grocery shopping, go home and put the food away, and still make Jacob's karate tournament by 2:00 p.m. When I got to Preston's apartment that Saturday, much more groomed than I usually am on the weekend, we went at it right away. In true romantic comedy fashion, we stumbled around the apartment in progressively giddy undress before falling onto his futon. After performing the sex act in several classic—but for me nearly forgotten—styles, I caught sight of his alarm clock and gave a cry that he mistook for pleasure. I had allotted time for married sex, not adulterous sex, and I was already late for Jacob's tournament. Obviously, Saturdays were going to be more complicated, schedule-wise, than I had envisioned.

That afternoon, as I sat, aching, on the hard bleachers, cheering on Jacob as he sparred, I told myself that having an extramarital affair was a common enough life experience. Not one I'd planned to have, surely, but it was too late for plans now. Besides, didn't I believe in fate? This affair with Preston was meant to be. Why else would my husband have suggested that I start attending the film society screenings? Why else had Preston been sitting right where I could admire his lupine hair and feel those first stirrings of lust? I had been sent to the theater expressly to find Preston because there was something I was meant to learn, to discover. It was some kind of test. I was going to grow. As a person.

The whistle blew, and we clapped as Jacob bowed to his opponent. My dalliance with Preston wouldn't hurt my family. I'd make sure my husband didn't find out, and anyway, I was sure it wouldn't last long. I just had to get Preston out of my system, and the only way I knew to get a man out of your system was to keep having sex with him until it didn't seem fun anymore. I figured you didn't *have* to be married to do that.

ABOUT TWO MONTHS PASSED, and the less I enjoyed the sex, the guiltier I felt. Tenderness crept in without my meaning for it to, and that worried me. Once or twice, I allowed myself to think what it would be like if I left my husband. I imagined sleeping every night in Preston's one-bedroom apartment, with the moldy shower curtain and the bicycle in the living room. I'd miss my pillowtop mattress and my matching blue Chinese ginger jar lamps. (I could bring them along, but Preston had no bedside tables.) I'd never again eat my husband's sweet potato pancakes with my children on Sunday morning. And how many years would it take to achieve the companionable silence I now enjoyed with my husband? I couldn't imagine returning to that phase when somebody was always saying, "What's wrong? Are you sure? You seem upset." It was like when somebody asked if I was going to have a third child and I thought about going back to all those diapers and sleepless nights.

So when Preston asked if my divorce was moving along, I'd say, "It's complicated. I don't want to talk about it." But that didn't satisfy him. He wanted to visit my father and play with my children; he was sure they would all become fond of him. They wouldn't, I promised. I assured him that they were difficult, opinionated people whom he didn't want to know. I reminded him to live in the moment. It didn't matter what I said, though—he pressed; he sulked. Obviously, I'd soon have to break up with him, but I didn't know the etiquette, and I liked having somewhere to go on Saturdays besides the nursing home. Plus, there was this one thing Preston did on that futon that my husband had never much gone for, and I wasn't quite ready to give it up.

Then my father took a turn for the worse. It was Valentine's week; the film was *Bringing Up Baby*. To my embarrassment, Preston brought me a red rose and put his arm around me during the screening. *If any of the film society people ever meet me in the grocery store with my husband,* I thought, *I'm going to be in big trouble.* At the bar afterward, we took our usual table. I explained that I wouldn't be able to come over that Saturday and that, no, he couldn't visit my father with me.

"You're my break from all that, Preston. You're my *Philadelphia Story*. You're my *Palm Beach Story*."

"I know it's probably been a long time since you've seen those movies," he pouted, "but you might recall that in both of them the husband and wife get back together."

I had to backpedal. Managing him had become too much like dealing with a touchy girlfriend—all hurt feelings and guesswork and apologies. "Oh, Preston. You know what I mean. Romance and all that. Good times. Black and white."

He clasped my hands on the tabletop, and I prayed nobody was watching. "But I want to be more than that," he said. "I want to be with you. I want to be *there* for you."

Behind the big windows of the restaurant, the street was slick with rain.

THE SATURDAY AFTER I told Preston I couldn't see him, I went by the library on my way to visit Daddy. When I'd visited him at lunch the day before, the X-rays had come back, confirming that he had pneumonia. Too weak to rearrange himself in the bed or cough up the stuff in his lungs, he hadn't been up for talking. All he could do was work on breathing, so I thought this time I'd just sit with him, even read to him if he liked.

At the library, I picked up a Czech novel I'd seen reviewed and a cookbook I thought would interest my husband. I dawdled among the shelves, looking for something I could read to Daddy. I hated seeing him the way he was now—his eyes yellowed, nails brittle, skin flaking. In the last few months, I could barely bring myself to touch him; a pat on the shoulder, a kiss on the forehead, or a brief hand squeeze was all I could manage. I'd back out of his room, throwing him bright promises of return, and then hurry to the visitors' bathroom to wash my hands with antibacterial soap and the hottest water I could stand.

I settled on a book about Churchill—"never, never, never give up" was one of my father's favorite sayings—and as I was checking out, my phone vibrated. Preston wanted me to come over for a "quick glass of wine." I reminded him I had to go see my father. It was the same excuse I gave my husband when I went to see Preston; now I was trying to use it to get *out* of seeing Preston.

"You have time for just one glass."

"All right. But no funny business."

"I love that you call it funny business."

By the time we made it out of the bedroom, it was nearly four o'clock, the time I was supposed to be back home.

"Damn it. I haven't even been to the nursing home yet." I struggled into my coat.

"What's the big deal?"

"I have a *family*, you know. I can't just *be gone* all the time."

"Okay." He frowned, uncertain how to take my anger. "But you're separated. You're allowed to *date*."

Uniform: You are running into danger.

"My father is really sick."

"I know that, sweetie, but I don't think it's fair for you to be mad at me because I invited you over for a glass of wine and made love to you—"

I can't stand to hear a man say "made love." It sounds so cheesy and sentimental.

"—You never said you had to be home at a certain time, and I don't think it's fair for you to be mad at me because you have scheduling problems."

He lay on his back, his hands clasped behind his head so that his elbows stuck out, the sheet draped to hide his junk. There was something so lazy and cavalier about him just then, his beady eyes roving over me as I dressed, that I got mad. It sounded like he was taunting me because he thought he was free and I was trapped.

"You know what, Preston? I think I'm getting sort of tired of you."

It was the first time I'd ever been mean to him, and I saw what went on in his face. He struggled not to say something mean back. I saw him think of mean things to say and dismiss them. I saw him decide to take the high road. Now, there is nothing I hate more, in an argument, than when somebody takes the high road. Because you know what people do up there on the high road? Look down on you. Look down on you, all smug, as you scream and shake your fist and dare them to come down and fight.

There were a hundred nasty things I wanted to say, but this time I took the high road myself. I told him I had to visit my sick father and go feed my children their supper. He didn't need to know that I don't do the cooking at my house. Properly chastened, he said that he understood. I kissed him to show we were made up and ran out to the car.

THREE WOMEN IN teal scrubs smoked in the parking lot, looking at their phones. Shift change. Inside, televisions blared, and the med techs moved in and out of doors doling out pills, worker bees in a hive of unmoving queens. I turned at the photo collage of residents, turned again at the framed poster of a Mary Cassatt mother and child, and hurried around Mrs. Beamon cradling her baby doll. Daddy's door was closed; he usually napped in the afternoon. Not wanting to wake him, I opened it just enough to see his bare freckled back. Bobby and a female attendant were bathing him or changing his diaper, so I softly closed the door again and leaned against the wall to wait.

After a few minutes, Bobby came out, gave me a sorrowful look, and put his hand on my arm. He'd never touched me before. I thought my father must be really bad off, and he wanted to prepare me for what I was about to see.

"We've got Mr. Charlie's shirt on him now, and I'll come back in a few minutes to shave him."

He spoke quietly, as though he didn't want anyone to hear. I wondered why he was continuing to pat my arm, shaking his head mournfully and moaning in gentle commiseration. Finally, it dawned on me to ask, "Are you saying—is he *dead*?"

His eyes widened, and he pulled back without letting go of my arm.

"Oh. I'm sorry! The nurse said she would call you." He shook his head again, this time at the ambient incompetence that suffused the place and made his job even harder. I reached for my phone. Then I realized how pointless it was to check my voicemail to find out what I already knew. Helpless, I held up my empty hands to Bobby. Now what?

He touched the door handle. "Do you want to see him?"

I nodded. Inside, the blinds were drawn against the fading afternoon, so the room was fairly dark. The female attendant cleared away the soiled diapers and the pan of water they'd used to wash him, then scurried out, mumbling her condolence. The head of the bed was raised to an angle between sitting up and lying down, as though Daddy was just relaxing to watch some TV. They'd buttoned

his blue-and-white-striped shirt at the throat, wet-combed his silver hair, and drawn the institutional blanket up to his sternum. His
mouth hung open, and without his dentures, his caved cheeks made
him look more gaunt than usual. He needed that shave Bobby was
going to give him, but all in all, he didn't look terrible for a man who
would have been eighty-one in a few months and who'd been sick a
long time.

"I'm just not hungry," he'd said on Thursday. "It hurts when I try to
put food in my stomach."

Whiskey: I require medical assistance.

I'd known he was dying, of course. I just hadn't wanted to think
about it.

I crossed to the bed and put my hand on his chest, thin and hard
under his shirt. If I knocked on it, I wondered, what kind of sound
would come?

"When?" I asked Bobby. Where had I been?

"Maybe forty-five minutes ago. Maybe an hour."

Preston's.

"Was he alone?" I undid the top button of Daddy's shirt, then the
second. Now he looked more comfortable, more natural.

"Yes. He was alone. I came in to check on him a while ago, and
the TV was off. That was strange because usually he turns it on at
lunchtime."

"He said he couldn't hear the screamer down the hall if the TV
was on."

Bobby nodded. "For a minute I thought he was asleep, but then I
saw."

Daddy's right hand hung out from under the blanket, dangling off the side of the bed. I remembered how I used to flop my arm off the top bunk at camp just to freak out the girl in the bunk below. "Oooh!" she'd squeal. "Stop it! It looks like a dead body's up there!"

"Was he feeling worse? Did he ask anybody to call me?" Was he mad because I wasn't there? That's what I really wanted to know. But Bobby had no answers. He approached the bed, took rubber gloves from a box on the hospital table, and put them on. "I think your father passed peacefully." He pushed the chin closed, then stood, holding my father's jaw, staring at the closed blinds. It struck me how many times Bobby must have helped people this way.

When I'd been there earlier in the week, Daddy had complained that his back was sore from lying around so much. Rubbing his shoulders through his nylon pajama shirt, I realized it was the first time I'd touched him that long in years.

"Oh, that feels so good," he'd sighed. "You used to beg to rub my back when you were a little girl. You were too small to do it hard enough." He scratched his whiskers with a thick, overgrown fingernail. "But it's the thought that counts."

I'd thought of Preston then. How simple was the thing I'd been seeking; it could have come from anybody. Ashamed, I had massaged Daddy's back until he said my arms must be getting tired and it was okay to stop.

"You don't have to hold his mouth closed," I told Bobby. "It doesn't bother me."

"Maybe if we do this."

He lowered the head of the hospital bed, then rolled up a hand towel and wedged it between Daddy's chin and chest. We agreed that was better. Bobby showed no impatience, but I knew he had work to do and told him he didn't need to stay with me. He bowed his head.

"I will pray for your father's soul to rest. And for you and your family."

"Thank you."

After Bobby left, I took my father's dangling hand and tucked it under the blanket. His stillness unnerved me. Now what? I rummaged in my purse for a notepad to start a list: Call the undertaker. Pack up Daddy's things. Call his brother down in Baton Rouge and his cousin in D.C. Write the obituary. But the problems weighing on me were not the ones I was writing down. I needed to call home.

"Oh, honey," said my husband, his voice breaking in sympathy. "I'll just drop off Jacob and Elsie at the Lawrences', and then I'll be right there."

"Don't tell them yet. I'll do it when I get home."

"All right."

"You know what I was thinking just now when I was calling you? I was thinking that if Daddy was the one making this call, you know, about me, or something, he would've flagged you. When you answered the phone, he would have said, 'Oscar.'"

"What's that mean?"

"Man overboard."

"Poor Charlie. At least you were there with him."

"But that's just it," I said, before I could chicken out. "I *wasn't* here."

There was a pause. Waiting for him to respond, I walked over to open the blinds, but it was 5:30 in February and already dark outside. I could smell the dinner trays out in the hall.

"Of course you were there," he said firmly.

From the pause, and the way he spoke, I realized he didn't want me to tell him anything. There would be no catharsis through confession. He was not going to indulge or absolve me, and my father, cooling on the bed, that towel under his chin, had gone where he could no longer help me, even if he'd been the kind to help, and I'd been the kind to ask.

Tooth

Tooth. Yellow as an old dog and twice as ugly. Pitted and scarred and smooth, too. With a jagged head and a fang of a root—one end like a human and one like a dog and hard to believe it could be either considering where Millie Minton found it. In her mouth, but not hers. Tooth in her mouth where teeth belong, but not hers. Her mouth and not her tooth. Now that was strange.

She wondered often if its owner—somewhere with a pit in his gum—it had to be a man's tooth—big as it was—she wondered if he smoked—yellow as it was and ugly, too.

Yellow as the creamed corn she found it in—even yellower in an old, bad, ugly way—yellow-stale and rancid. Really it seems like it would have stuck out to her eye, that she'd have seen it before she put it smack in her mouth. Just sitting in her corn—bigger than corn and harder, too.

Crunched right down on it like it was her own tooth. A strange feeling biting tooth not your own.

Spit it in her napkin, took a sip of tea to wash that peculiar crunch out of her mouth. But she could still hear that grinding in her head—that grit resistance—hard tooth in among the soft corn, just waiting.

Yellow as an old dog and twice as ugly. Now that's like something Old Mister would say—just like. Doesn't he always say to her, you're fat as an old sow and twice as ugly—and just laughs. Thinks everything is more funny if you say twice as ugly. That just about kills him laughing. He really enjoys that.

Old Mister. Not her daddy, but her daddy's daddy. Not even her mama's daddy, but Millie's daddy's daddy. What were they keeping that old man for?

Nobody noticed her with that tooth—spitting in her napkin and saving it. Her mama didn't notice—too busy eating and crying, eating and crying. Old Mister didn't notice—too busy eating and cussing, cussing and eating. And now she's had that tooth a while—a long while—eight, nine years or more—and it sits in her dresser drawer, underneath her underwear—under, under, like a treasure.

One thing for sure, she never would tell her mother or Old Mister either. He had his own teeth—a whole set to go in and out. Stayed in a glass of water when he didn't want them.

Once she wrote to the canning company to ask what they thought. How does a tooth get into a can of creamed corn and what kind of tooth did they think it was and what did they plan to do about it, thank you? She waited and waited. Finally she did get a letter with a row of crops printed at the top—a sun setting on them—and they said they didn't know and they sure were sorry and how about a case of vegetables? How about a lifetime supply of creamed corn and field peas and some French-cut green beans, too, if she wanted, because here at SunDale we value each and every one of our customers.

Could somebody possibly lose a tooth and not notice? Could you really bend over the line at the SunDale vegetable processing plant and a huge old ugly tooth just fall out of your mouth? Wouldn't you have to spit it in there deliberately? Wouldn't you just have to spit? Just have to?

Somebody did it for a joke. It was a good joke, too—better than anything Old Mister said twice as ugly about, better than her daddy running off and not coming back—her mama always said he thought that was a good joke but they never thought it was so funny. But to throw a tooth—spit a tooth—in a vat of creamed corn and imagine it sealed up and shipped out. Then one day some poor fool opens the can, pours the corn in a pot—heat, serve, and just eating along until crack—Tooth! In your mouth, but not your tooth! Now that's a *funny* joke. That's something you could laugh on for a long time.

Millie liked to think one day she would meet the person who had lost that tooth. One day she'd be talking to a stranger, and she'd notice he was missing one. She'd just happen to have it with her, and she'd pull

it out and say, *Look here.* Look what I've got. Haven't you been wondering where this got to?

The one date she'd had since she turned thirty, that one man, he'd
had some pretty teeth—white as breath mints and twice as sweet.
But who ever had a chance at love with Old Mister reclining in
his chair, watching John Wayne at high volume and barking or-
ders? What chance for love with her mother crying and waiting,
waiting and crying? What chance on the itchy horsehair sofa and
Old Mister barking and Mama crying and John Wayne always in
trouble?

It put her mind to violence. Maybe that tooth was part of a victim—
dismembered and dismantled so good that nobody could ever put
it together. Some clever murderer walked scot-free and all over the
land—in butterbeans—in black-eyed peas—in stewed tomatoes—
a fingernail, an eyelid, a smidge of tendon. Somewhere those twenty-
seven others—eye teeth, incisors, molars. Thirty-one, counting
wisdom.

What chance for love with Old Mister barking?

Sometimes when Millie got to feeling low, she'd rummage among her
cotton briefs, feeling for that slick, odd little thing—and then her
hand would light on it and she'd think what in the world? How did I
ever find this and how did it find me and who lost it and why did it
end up in my corn—on my dinner plate and in my mouth—now in
my underwear drawer? Maybe I am chosen for something.

Old Mister always wanting a ride someplace and Millie sweating to death in the hot car, waiting and sweating, sweating and waiting, while he put his teeth in. Vanity, said the preacher. Like he had somebody to look good for. And what chance for Millie?

Old Mister was just a little bitty old dried-up thing. Not big as a minute—only five-six now with that hump in his back. One hundred pounds and almost as old. Could eat his weight in a week. Wouldn't anybody miss him if he wasn't there.

She'd thought on it a hundred times and it made her laugh a little in her mind, thinking it but no good way to do it. Daddy's daddy, not her daddy. One gone, and one to go. Always wanting a ride. When it came to her it was a surprise, a gift, and before she thought about it, he was in there, hollering, but muffled, like in a well.

Only took half a minute to pick him up, set him in the trunk and slam it shut. Thirty seconds from ground to trunk. So surprised he barely had time to struggle.

Weak little old man struggle—dry bones shifting in a sack.

Drove the car into the garage and shut the door. Two doors between them. Went in the house. Three doors. In her room. Four doors now. Her mama out shopping at the store.

Hottest day of the summer. Hundred degrees in the shade. And him, a hundred pounds, if that.

At supper, her mama says where's Old Mister and Millie shrugs and says, "Beats me."

Mama on the phone calling, and Millie says to her—what do you care? He isn't even your daddy. Daddy's daddy. Not yours, not mine.

Dreams all her teeth fall out and she's got nothing but bloody mush-mouth. Dreams so many teeth in her mouth and none of them hers. Crunching on teeth, spitting them out—rapid-fire bones shooting. Teeth, but not her teeth. Her mouth, but not her teeth.

Skin dry as old paper, flaky like fish and smells twice as bad. Rattle-cough, meanness, mucus, cussing and eating, eating and cussing. Don't miss him now and won't miss him later. Daddy's daddy, not her daddy.

Tooth. Dull dagger-root. Sitting in the underwear drawer, under like treasure. Smoked yellow. Flesh-rot ringed. Hard as a rock and twice as old. Old as the hills and twice as ugly.

Et tu, Miss Jones?

———

Mr. Andrews used to let me sit in the brown leather arm-chair next to his desk in the back of his antique shop and pore over his provenances while he typed. About seventy, tall, thin, he always wore khaki pants, a pressed Oxford shirt, and a cardigan in a fatherly color like burgundy or olive. He'd opened his shop not long before my folks closed theirs, but I didn't get to know him until after they'd died. Having been raised among old things, I found the sight and smell of antiques soothing, and the wet spring after my mother died, I was drawn to wander the shops on South Elm, talking to the dealers who'd known her and my father when they were healthy and funny and sexy and bright.

The antiques dealers on South Elm were a motley guild—bickering couples, hoarders hemmed in by piles of mouse-infested junk, empty nesters who consoled themselves with arranging dried flowers and lovingly polishing the furniture with beeswax. Like family, they gossiped and fell out from time to time, but they also warned each other about shoplifters and check bouncers. When one of their number sickened, they helped out; when one died, they awaited the auction with gloomy anticipation. The auction is the antique dealer's real funeral, where his life's choices are held up one by one and submitted to judgment, like deeds recited to Saint Peter.

Mr. Andrews, unfailingly polite, never asked me when I was going to get around to selling my parents' belongings, and soon his was the only shop I visited on Saturday mornings. I found charming his wavy silver hair and long patrician fingers, spatulate at the tips from years at the piano. A retiree—he never said from what—and a widower (her name was Martha), he taught piano as a means of supplementing his income. Around 11:00, our conversation would be interrupted by a child clutching sheet music, and though Mr. Andrews welcomed me to look around until the lesson was finished, I could never bear the strained, halting sound of a person learning to play (myself included, years ago), and I always left.

The furniture in his shop was the mishmash you find so many places: Victorian chairs in chewed velvet or threadbare needlepoint, Edwardian chests of drawers with buckled veneer, loose-jointed pine tables, country washstands shedding paint. My mother had been an expert on furniture, but because we didn't often like the same things, I always doubted my own taste and felt safer admiring smalls. At Mr. Andrews's place, every surface was covered with smalls: porcelain figurines, glassware, silver spoons, inlaid wooden boxes, cloisonné lamps, stoneware jars, and iron kitchen implements.

Nearby shops carried similar items in the same profusion. What distinguished Mr. Andrews's stock was how he labeled it. While other dealers slapped on a price sticker (Imari plate, $150), Mr. Andrews typed up a detailed provenance for each item.

The paper was delicious, as buttery in the hands as good pastry in the mouth: ivory cotton linen, 24 lb., with a crown watermark. Elegantly printed at the top was the shop's name; underneath, in smaller letters: *Jeremiah Andrews, Proprietor.* The typing was rotten—page-long, single-spaced paragraphs with errors xxed out and capitals P, B, and W staggering toward the line above or below—but you understood when you saw his ancient Royal. It was the sort of heavy, black, delightfully clackety typewriter you see in photos of modernist writers. I was amazed how fast he could get along on it. Once I asked to try, and it was murder getting the keys to go down.

For the most important objects, he filled manila file folders with photocopied pictures of similar items, along with articles from the *Smithsonian* or the *New York Times,* maps and census records, even genealogies. But the stories themselves were what appealed to me.

How, for example, he'd driven down a country lane one Sunday afternoon and spied three wild dogs drinking rainwater from a basin in the weedy grass. He'd stopped, pulled a pistol from under his seat (a detail hard to reconcile with his avuncular cardigans), gotten out, and fired a shot to scatter the dogs. The basin turned out to be the top section of a baptismal font, blackened with soot. The dogs paced at a distance; he fired again, and this time they ran off into the woods and didn't return. After finding the font too heavy to lift, he'd wandered the country roads looking for the vandalized church from which it might have come, then stopped at a gas station to inquire among its grizzled habitués. He was interested in old churches, he said. Were there any nearby?

They knew of a Baptist church that practiced full submersion— "down by the riverside," a dunking and a hearty picnic, no font in sight—and a small Episcopal church that had burned in the last year. He'd followed their colorful directions to a rectangle of bare earth surrounded by high grass. The brick piers still stood at intervals, the wood frame they'd supported gone. Behind the scorched footprint, neglected graves were drowning by generations in the soft, heaving dirt. He recalled how he'd gone back to the gas station and hired two dubious-looking characters to come lift the font into the trunk of his car.

"You couldn't have written to the diocese?" I asked. "Offered to return it?"

Hunting and pecking with his forefingers, he peered studiously over the black ribbon at his work. "I'm not a religious man, Miss Jones." Always Miss Jones, not Adelia, and certainly never Delia, which nobody has called me since Daddy died. He used to sing to me, *Delia girl how I love you and I wish I could take your place,* and Mama would look affronted and say, "I never would've named that child that if I'd known you were going to sing her that song all the time. You do know the Delia in that song is a *prostitute*? And the singer *shot her?*" Then Daddy would say, "You're not a snob, honey, but you do a fine imitation of one." And she'd bump him with her hip and say, "I just don't think that's a nice song to sing to a little girl, that's all."

Mr. Andrews cleaned the font, set it on a concrete pillar by the door, and filled it with candies. Whenever I reached for a butterscotch or peppermint, I recalled the dogs, the pistol, the country roads, the sinking graves. Like many things in the shop, his glorified candy dish was not for sale. I never asked whether his attachment was to the objects themselves or to the tales he'd written about them. I understood they couldn't be separated.

ONE SATURDAY IN early summer, I went to the farmers' market and bought sweet potato jacks, these terribly fattening but terribly delicious fritters. With my poor appetite, if I felt like eating a thing, I ate it. I bought coffees, too, and went to see Mr. Andrews. When he finished his fritter, he licked his fingers, watching me with those lovely blue eyes, and lit a cigarette. Had we been closer in age, I'd have wanted to date him. My best friend Eleanor, who'd never met Mr. Andrews, referred to him as "your boyfriend." I said huffily that I was aware that in befriending this older man, I was seeking solace for the loss of my parents, and Eleanor said there was nothing wrong with that.

When he'd finished his cigarette, he opened a desk drawer and pulled out a small, thick jar. The top was sealed on with old wax, and inside was a murky, brownish liquid. Settled at the bottom was a waxy oblong thing, yellowish, whorled in the middle and weirdly familiar.

Right then, a little girl came in with her music. As Mr. Andrews hurried to put the jar away, I wondered if it contained something obscene he didn't want her to see. He handed me a blue three-ring binder.

"For you, Miss Jones. Be sure to bring this back next week," he said, taking my elbow and almost pushing me to the door. I was excited. Never before had he shown me a provenance important enough to have its own notebook. As soon as I got outside, I opened it.

The first page read: THE AMPUTATEXD EAR OFX VINCENT VAN XGOGH

That evening I had my friend Irene over to dinner. Usually, we met in a coffee shop or a bar, but I was trying not to be so cocooned in grief, and inviting anybody other than Eleanor to my house felt, in those sad reclusive days, like a great act of daring. I cleaned all day, and by the time Irene arrived, a little after 7:00, the house looked better than it had in years. Irene didn't apologize for being late. She hugged me, then walked around the living room with a glass of the chardonnay she'd brought, plucking at her gauzy purple scarf and examining my pictures and books.

"All these old things, Adelia. I don't know anything about antiques except I'm supposed to like them."

I asked how her work was going. A literature professor, she was always eager to talk about her research, and I welcomed the distraction, asking her enough questions over the trout and salad to ensure we never got around to discussing me. Irene's undergraduate degree had been in psychology, and she was interested in science as well as religion, art, and politics, so our conversations were delightfully wide ranging. One of the courses she taught was on the Bible as literature. She'd begun to make an interdisciplinary specialty of diagnosing literary characters with various disorders and hypothesizing how their conditions influenced their actions. Just then she was working on a paper in which she claimed that certain biblical personages suffered developmental delays from being born to older mothers.

"Look at how placidly Isaac goes to the sacrifice! 'Where's the lamb, daddy?' and Abraham says, 'Don't worry, son, God will provide the lamb.' Wink, wink. Yeah, God's providing a nice juicy lamb, all right. And the boy lets himself be tied up. He must know by then that he's going to have his throat cut, he's going to be burnt up—and he doesn't ever struggle? That's not normal."

"He's a child." I shrugged. "Children follow their parents."

"Your father ties you up, puts you on a rock, brandishes a knife over you? I think you're going to scream or try to get up and make a run for it."

"He's a child in a completely patriarchal society," I pointed out. "Conditioned to be obedient." (Obedience is the point of the story, I was thinking, but I didn't want to accuse her of missing the obvious.) "And how old is he?"

"It never says."

"See. He could be three years old. He's totally trusting."

"I'm thinking maybe autism? Lack of affect. I mean, he sees his father getting ready to do this horrible thing, and he never protests? It's a foundational trauma. I'll address that in my paper, of course, and explain how it informs the struggle toward nation building between Jacob and Esau. Their mother—Rebecca—was old, too, of course, and we know that women over thirty-five tend to have higher incidences of multiple births. Mmm. This is good cheese."

"Smoked Gouda," I said. I found her powerful appetite encouraging and had more myself.

"I read somewhere that children of older fathers tend to be more depressive, bipolar, that kind of thing," I offered. "Maybe you could use that? Maybe Isaac was suicidal from a young age?"

Shaking a piece of cheese at me, she said it wasn't a bad idea. I felt pleased and slightly ashamed. I enjoyed speculating with Irene, but her work struck me as an intellectual fool's errand, worse than quixotic. By *worse,* I mean that it had none of Quixote's tragic dignity. Her ideas, when put on paper, were so limited and her way of expressing them so baroque and lifeless. She had obtained her doctorate, however, and I hadn't, so maybe there was something profound in her scholarship that I just wasn't theoretical-minded enough to grasp.

After dinner, we sat on the sofa, drinking wine and eating chocolate. It was May, and the windows were open, admitting happy neighborhood sounds and a warm breeze. We had moved on to comparing ex-boyfriends. Then she saw the blue binder on the coffee table. Was that something I was working on? An editing project? A novel?

In my worry over getting everything ready for my guest, I'd forgotten all about the binder. I told her about Mr. Andrews's shop, about his fascinating provenances and how far-fetched they could be. She opened the binder and read the front page.

"He has the thing in a jar," I said.

"Maybe *he* cut it off somebody," she said, shaking her head as she turned the pages.

I thought about how easily he pushed down the sticky keys on that Royal.

"Does he seriously think he's got Vincent Van Gogh's actual frickin' ear?"

"Don't do that," I pleaded, regretting having exposed him to her scorn. "He's very kind to me."

I pushed the binder under the sofa, and though she changed the subject, the incident had broken the easy mood of the evening. When

Irene left, earlier than I'd expected, I poured more wine and settled down to read Mr. Andrews's story.

YEARS AGO, HE had met a Mr. Turner, whose father had been raised in Polynesia in the 1890s. When Turner père died, his elderly brother came to the funeral in Washington, and for the first time, Turner fils heard the tale of how the two brothers, as boys in fin de siècle Polynesia, had fetched drinks, groceries, and supplies for a French painter who lived nearby. One day, the painter—drunk and finding no ready coin in the house—had tipped them with the jar and the accompanying tale that the ear within had belonged to another artist, who'd cut it off himself in a frenzy and sent it to a woman he desired.

Only years later did the brothers realize to whom the ear must have belonged, but by then they'd misplaced the jar. The uncle had recently found it in his attic and, having no children himself, had brought it to his nephew. It was up to Turner fils to decide what to do with it, the uncle considering himself too old for the public commotion that such a revelation inevitably would bring.

Mr. Turner didn't believe his uncle's tale, but he was willing to sell the jar as an oddity. For Mr. Andrews, though, the story had the ring of truth. (I chuckled at the idea of him weighing the plausibility of another man's outlandish story.) Artists were indeed wild, unpredictable creatures. Only one point troubled him. By all known accounts, shortly before Van Gogh cut off his ear, he'd brandished a razor at Gauguin, who'd fled, never to see his mad friend again. Why then, Mr. Andrews wondered, hadn't the severed ear rotted out back of the French bordello where it had frightened a tormented woman into a faint?

He pondered the question for years until he read a review (a copy was in the binder) of a book in which German historians proposed that it was Gauguin himself who sliced off his friend's ear with a fencing sword in self-defense that nasty night in Arles, two days before Christmas. According to the historians, the painters had concocted the story of self-mutilation; Gauguin had stuck with it out of remorse, Van Gogh out of shame. Gauguin must have retrieved the ear from the prostitute Rachel, Mr. Andrews wrote, and kept it as a talisman of his guilt, even as he was living it up in his island paradise.

On the internet, I found that the German historians' theory had been immediately debunked by the Van Gogh Museum. Another scholar posited that Vincent had cut off his own ear in despair because he'd found out that his brother Theo, who was supporting him, planned to marry. The next morning, I checked out a stack of books from the university library, and for several days, I read Vincent's letters to Theo. Falling into a fugue state of fascination, I learned about his life among and away from other artists, about his religious obsession and his black despair. I gazed at reproductions of paintings I'd never bothered to look at before. It wasn't their subjects that moved me but the colors. Jeweled, muddy, however they came, I steeped myself in his colors, so captivated that I forgot to go to bed at night and fell asleep on the sofa.

It didn't worry me that the thing in the jar resembled *a whole ear,* à la *Blue Velvet,* when everybody said that Van Gogh had cut off only part of a lobe. Insistence on provable fact didn't come into my thinking anymore. On Saturday, Mr. Andrews and I spread open the books, pointed out our favorite paintings, and discussed passages from the brothers' letters. It was raining, and nobody came into the cozy, dimly lit shop to bother us. I grew so comfortable that I kicked off my shoes, something I'd never done there before. He didn't mind. Maybe he was a charlatan or a madman or the dumbest innocent. Perhaps, in a way, he was all three. It didn't matter. There was something about that shop I believed in, something about that dear old man I loved.

IN THE DAYS that followed, he showed me wonderful things, including a dried, brittle skin shed by the asp that dealt Cleopatra her fatal bite. Going too far? Still, I listened. Before long, I could see the fang glinting at her bosom.

IRENE KEPT ASKING me to take her antiquing, and I kept putting her off. Since my parents had died, I'd only gone down to South Elm alone. One midsummer day, though, we were walking together in the park near my house. She was encouraging me, not for the first time, to go back to school.

"You've got to do something, Adelia. It's not good for a woman to have no work, even if you can afford it."

My mother's estate wasn't yet settled, but my older sister, who was the executor, had let me take an advance on my inheritance because I was having trouble finding a job. Her disapproval was nothing new, so I pretended it didn't bother me.

"I can't afford it," I said. "Not much longer."

"It's not good to isolate yourself when you're depressed," Irene said. "Believe me, I've been there."

We walked in silence for a few minutes, watching the runners and strollers going by, the dogs on leashes. She had not "been there." Her parents were still putting up a Christmas tree every year and annoying her with the frequency of their phone calls. She had a career and a boyfriend with a career, and she didn't cut her own hair with a plastic razor or hide in the kitchen when her neighbor rang the doorbell.

"Let's go downtown, and you can show me around the junk shops," she said, linking my arm with hers in a chummy manner I resented. "I want to get my mother a cool birthday gift, and since you know so much about all that stuff, you can keep me from making a mistake."

She had no real intention of buying a gift, but I didn't care. The opportunity to feel intellectually superior to her, even for a moment, was irresistible.

At shop after shop, I pointed out true antique versus reproduction—*gold v. dross,* my mother used to say, the phrase like the name of a lawsuit. I didn't care if I sounded pedantic or pretentious. Irene listened but seemed as uninterested after the lesson as before, and once, after urging her to pick up a piece of lead glass to feel its heft, I noticed her cleaning her fingers with hand sanitizer and tissues.

As we approached Mr. Andrews's place, we heard the piano playing. You had to lift the handle and push the door hard—otherwise, it wouldn't budge—and when I opened it, the bells at the top jangled violently. A spotty teenaged boy stared at me from the piano bench, his hands suspended above the keys, the broken music hanging between us.

Mr. Andrews nodded, and the boy resumed. He played beautifully, with real feeling. I can't say what the piece was, but I'd guess Romantic period. Brooding stuff, like the roilsome bruised sky of a Caspar David Friedrich landscape, it added very much to the impression I hoped the shop would make on Irene, who was picking up one of the provenances. As she read, I found myself watching her face for signs of skepticism or pleasure, and I wondered why I was so anxious for her to approve of the shop and Mr. Andrews and, by extension, me.

The boy finished playing and shambled out. Mr. Andrews came toward us, smiling, his long hand outstretched. I introduced Irene.

"Ah, Madame Junior Professor," he said. "Enchanté."

"I've been wanting to come see your shop. Adelia tells me your things often have rather surprising stories behind them."

I saw at once that the visit could only sour. First, she challenged something he'd written about a bust of Benjamin Franklin, and they had a strained but civil argument about that. He kept calling her "Madame Junior Professor." She used phrases like "in layman's terms" or "for a person not in academia, it might be difficult to . . ." I watched, speechless and queasy, until they reached a stalemate. Then Madame Junior Professor (it was hard to call her anything else in my head after he'd said it so often) dropped a snide remark about Van Gogh's ear. Mr. Andrews looked at me, plainly hurt. He held up his elegant forefinger.

"Wait one moment."

While he went in the back, Irene and I stood at opposite ends of the shop, pretending to be engrossed, she with her phone, me with a book I'd picked up. I didn't know what to say to her. This was one reason I hadn't wanted to bring her here: she hadn't been raised, as I had, not to argue with people. As far as she was concerned, the whole world was her arena. She was sure to provoke him further when he came back, and though part of me admired how intrepid she was, I was already trying to think how to apologize for her.

He reappeared from behind the curtain and handed her a dagger with a jeweled hilt. As she examined it, he rifled in his desk, then offered her a file. Embarrassed for him now, I wanted to snatch the file out of her hands, but she'd already opened it. She read for only a minute before tossing it down.

"That's bullshit," she said, holding her purse to her chest. I thought it a strange defensive gesture, and I didn't like her cussing at him. Yet he didn't seem to need my defense; instead of looking cowed or confused, his expression verged on smug.

"My provenance is no more specious than your supposition that Abraham's little Isaac was—a what? A mongoloid?"

She clucked at his outdated terminology and gaped at me. "Is *that* what you told him?"

"Not in those words—not that word. I thought your research would interest him. I mean, *I* think it's fascinating."

I moved to pick up the folder, but slowly, for there was barely enough room to squeeze between the furniture crowded with china and glass. Growing up in my parents' shop, it was always, *Watch out! Be careful!* All my life had been spent trying not to knock over things that might break and couldn't be replaced. I was tired of it.

Inside the folder was the familiar ivory letter paper.

THE DAGGER WITH WXICH ABRAHAM NEARLY DIXSPATCHED ISAAC

"You're just making things up!" Irene said. "My work is a way of understanding our diseased Western culture from its very beginnings. There are a lot of theoretical underpinnings that might not make sense to you—"

He played a careless arpeggio on the upright. "I'm sure your theories will be a great success in the ivory tower. What could appeal more to your academic friends than for you to discover that the authority of the Bible—the basis, after all, for so much of our diseased Western culture—rests on the actions of mentally unsound people?"

I'd never seen her look so unsure of herself, and that was when I made a terrible mistake: I laughed. I couldn't help it.

Irene stalked to the door. When it wouldn't open for her, Mr. Andrews, usually so courtly, made no move to help. I hurried to let her out. She walked so fast along the sidewalk that I almost had to run to keep up.

"Irene, I'm sorry. *I'm sorry.*"

The people we passed quickly averted their eyes, as though we were quarreling lovers who ought to keep our troubles private.

"He's just playing," I said, reaching to touch her arm.

She jerked away, pressing her lips together in her effort not to cry. She wasn't as tough as she pretended to be.

"And what about you, Adelia? Are you *playing*? I don't even know what you mean by that. I can't even talk to you right now."

I've never known how to answer people when they act cold. She drove away, leaving me without a ride. Back inside the shop, Mr. Andrews had switched on the radio to a jazz station and was making tea with his electric kettle.

"You wrote that after I told you about her paper," I said.

He put his hand to his chest, feigning hurt. "Et tu, Miss Jones?"

"Wrong dagger."

He turned his back and fussed with his tea things. The kettle burbled, steam fuming from its spout. On the radio, the high hat hissed and jigged. Then the saxophone broke in.

"I don't know why you want to hang around such people, Miss Jones. Philistines in freethinkers' clothing. Literalists. Everything cause and effect. It's absurd. As if the world can be reduced to that."

I DIDN'T REPLY to an accusatory email from Irene, and I avoided South Elm the next weekend, and the next, and the next. I couldn't make the choice I felt they were pressing me to make, and in failing to decide, I began, to my surprise, to feel the relief, the lightness I'd so long been wanting. I took to going to the movies on Saturdays. Sometimes I went with Eleanor, who was always glad to get away from her husband and kids for a few hours. One day over lunch she remarked that perhaps I'd brought the junior professor to meet Mr. Andrews because I missed hearing my parents fight with each other. Later, thinking about her theory, I decided it was wrong. I didn't miss hearing their fighting at all.

ONCE HE'D LET me purchase, cheaply, a box of cut-up magazines "from the estate of Joseph Cornell." After I stopped visiting him, I used to leaf through books, looking at images of Cornell's collages, trying to find something in them that matched the empty windows in my magazines.

AT THE DRUGSTORE, I ran into a friend of Mama's who touched my hand with hers, now wrinkled and liver spotted. Who else remembers her in those strapless yellow sundresses and white tennis skirts that made all our fathers stop to watch her coming and going?

"You know what I really miss about your mom? Long after all our other friends were jaded by their divorces and their jobs and their children—whatever had disappointed them—your mom would read a book or hear about something on television or go to an art exhibit and come back enchanted. Just *enchanted* that the world had such wonders in it."

I FINALLY RETURNED to South Elm this fall, hunting an out-of-print book I wanted to give Eleanor. I was working again, and I was glad that I could tell people I was busy. I was seeing a new guy, too, and I could imagine what Mr. Andrews would have said about him—*surely you've had enough of the professoriate, Miss Jones?*

Mr. Andrews's shop was locked up, and in the window was a sign picturing a bunch of superheroes: "Comic Relief—Coming Soon!" The other dealers told me he had cancer, Parkinson's; opinions differed. His daughter had moved him to wherever she lived, and the shop had been rented again, but the contents were to be auctioned off if I was interested.

It happened on a drizzly, chill November morning. The auction house smelled of dust and wet clothes. No mention of the provenances was made. I bid on a stand with a sweetly scalloped apron but had to drop out when the price went too high. I watched the new owner pay and inspect the stand. He opened the drawer, pulled out a piece of paper, balled it up, and tossed it on the floor. I started to go tell him what he was throwing away, but then I saw how he grabbed the stand under the apron, without love, and carried it one-handed toward the exit.

The Woman Who
Did Things Wrong

The first thing the woman got wrong was the birth. She knew as soon as the sharp-fingered nurse pronounced her progress inadequate, her dilation limited. New nurse, new shift, sun feebly rising behind metal blinds: still no baby.

Time was wasting. When they broke her water, a wet warmth soaked out beneath her, all her life's shame undammed and dripping to the vinyl floor.

(*I birthed at home,* other women later told her, smug over wine on a rare girls' night, none of them girls anymore and the nights both longer and shorter. *Surrounded by candles,* they said, *like in that movie. In that movie,* the woman said, *the candles were for fucking in the middle of, not for pushing a giant-headed baby out of your vagina.* The other women laughed. *Something's always wanting in or out of that thing,* she said, to hear them laugh again. That they craved vulgarity when drunk was her favorite thing about the other women.)

By the time the doctor cut her open like a bad wolf, she'd almost forgotten that the prize for her endurance would be a baby. And when at last the nurse offered the bloody gift to its father—another thing she'd gotten wrong—the woman wondered if by mistake they'd carved her blue-red heart right out of her. She'd never imagined it would cry like that and was relieved when they took it away.

The woman was poked and dosed and put in a clean bed. When they brought the baby to feed, she got that wrong, too. She had to be taught. When they came with forms and insisted on a name, she couldn't stop changing her mind. Her indecision, she knew, incensed her husband, though he pretended it didn't. To appease him, she agreed to name the baby after his mother.

At home with the child, she wondered what she had gotten herself into. She fed and washed, rocked and sang, knowing there must be better foods, better songs. The night, when she was too exhausted to sleep, was when the baby seemed most likely to die. Daily, her terror lost its bright edge, which only made it more worrisome. A dull knife, she knew, is the most dangerous, how it glances off its target to slice the hand instead. Sometimes when the baby cried, she had to walk away.

The baby grew into a girl and was healthy. Happy, too, except when she started school, and when her parents split up, and when she had to go on weekends to her father's house, where the food was bad, the bedtime early. As the girl got older, she found it harder and harder to stop her tears. She cried when she had to ride a bus or take a test, when she had to eat eggs or wash her hair. Even though the woman suspected she must have done something to make her daughter so unhappy, she took the girl to doctors, hoping they would find another cause. None of them could locate the source of the trouble. At last, the mother felt forced to admit what she already knew—that she'd passed her old terror on to her daughter, who suffered so aw-fully because for her the terror was new and sharp.

Now the mother's own terror returned, doubling the terror in the house. Now, thought the terror, it was getting somewhere. Impressed with itself, it swelled into room after room, stockpiling itself in cor-ners like grain or gold in an older, better story. The woman and the girl did not know what to do.

Then one day a letter slipped through the mail slot and slapped the floor.

Far away, the woman read, her mother lay ill.

(The old woman had a telephone but preferred letters for sharing bad news. She hated to hear people crying on the line.)

The woman went to her daughter, who lay under seven blankets in her dark room.

"We must make the journey to see Grandmother."

"I can't."

"We must."

"I can't."

Beneath the blankets, the girl trembled.

"Look," the woman said. She too feared the packing of suitcases and making of arrangements. What if she forgot to lock the house? What if she wrecked the car? Mistakes lurked everywhere, waiting for her to make them. But she must visit her sick mother.

The woman said, "We will just have to get fiercer."

"How will we do that?" the girl asked.

The woman thought and thought. She consulted her books. (She had the internet but preferred books. Books did not have a comments section.) But the books gave her no clear answer.

She decided to chance it. She said, "I think we must let in the wind."

The woman opened the windows. The wind rushed in, smelling like allergens and speeding cars and men with madness on their minds.

"Close them!" the girl begged.

"Wait," the woman said, trembling too.

The wind stripped off the girl's seven blankets. It ripped around the corners of the rooms and scattered the terror like dry leaves. It tangled the mother's hair and reminded her of a good time long ago.

After a few minutes, they got used to the wind. After an hour, going out into the wind felt possible.

Soon their bags were packed, the house was locked, and the mother eased the car onto the road, where the other drivers' impatient honking reminded her of the girl's father. She said so, to make her daughter laugh. But the girl wasn't ready. She only felt up to smiling a little.

They drove for three hours until they reached the forsaken county where the grandmother lived. Here the road climbed, winding and switching back around the sheer rock faces of the mountainsides. Theirs was a new kind of hardness for the daughter, who marveled at how the earth fell away on one side of the road and stretched into the clouds on the other.

The grandmother lived at the end of a quiet path snaking down through pine woods. Her house sat like a surprise in the middle of a meadow. Through the meadow ran the cool, ancient river that had cut the valley and left it green.

Though small and untidy, the house shone. The woman had forgotten how much sunlight could get into a house. The grandmother staggered up from her bed, eager to welcome them, the skin of her kissed cheek translucent as a paper lantern. She begged them eat and drink to refresh themselves after their long journey, but the food in the cupboard had spoiled. The woman left the girl to sit with the grandmother while she went to see what could be bought at the store up the road.

Because she'd been alone for so long, the grandmother wanted to talk. As the girl listened, she noticed that although the sun was going down, a pale yellowish light suffused the room. When the old woman shuffled toward the door to let out her cat, the golden glow both followed her and shone everywhere, and the girl wondered how the same light could be in two places at once.

When the mother returned with groceries, the grandmother said what they needed was soup. Because she was too weak to make it herself, the woman and the girl would have to prepare it according to her instructions.

"Just show us the recipe," the girl said.

"Oh, no," the grandmother said. She would make up the soup as she went along.

It started, of course, with an onion.

As the woman washed the vegetables and the girl chopped, the grandmother told them about all the soups she knew: soup to calm fever, soup to balm sadness, soup to give courage, soup to make someone fall in love with you.

"Where did you learn to make up so many soups?" the girl asked.

The grandmother said, "From my mother, how else?"

At the mention of her mother's mother, a rusty grief pricked the woman. She scrubbed harder the carrot she was washing and tried to push the grief away. Surely no good could come of remembering her nana's warm kitchen or the perfume of her face cream after so many years. Why cry again?

All of a sudden, the girl dropped her knife and cried out.

"*Oh!*"

She held her hand aloft. For a moment all anybody could see was a thin red line. Then the red line began to bubble and widen. The mother took her daughter in her arms and let go of the tears she'd been saving. As the mother's tears fell, the trickle of blood from the daughter's hand became a stream, then a gush, and soon tears and blood puddled and swirled across the kitchen floor. Soon they were ankle deep in foaming pink, but the mother found she could not stop crying. Nor did the girl's blood cease to run.

The flood of bloody tears rose to their knees, then their waists. It pulled Grandmother up out of her chair, and she bobbed along, turning slowly like an apple. The grandmother began to laugh.

"Why are you laughing, Granny?" the girl cried.

"Oh, Mother," the woman said, holding on to the drowning cupboard. "What should we do?"

The grandmother needed no book to tell her the answer.

"Open the windows," she said. "Swim."

They did what she said. The rosy tide swept the three swimmers over the windowsills, carrying them along on the ferrous, salty swell of a great wave. For a moment or two, being carried was all they knew. Then the great wave crested, fell, and deposited them into the meadow before running off to join the river.

The three gasping women flopped and twitched in the wet grass. When they were sure the ground beneath them wasn't going anywhere, they calmed and fell still. They lay on their backs and stared up as the last of the bloody water receded.

The sky was black now and the stars had come, white. Back in the wood, a hooey owl couldn't stop himself explaining.

Not understanding his language, the girl asked her grandmother what had happened.

"I never know," was the answer.

The mother asked if they'd been reborn.

"No," said the grandmother, "that bloody business only happens once."

Together they watched the white stars shine, silent as stones.

After a while the mother asked, "How was I born?"

"On a flood just like that," said the grandmother. "Except with a little shit mixed in."

The girl laughed. *Shit* still made her laugh when somebody said it out loud.

The mother laughed, too, because her daughter's laughter always made her.

The grandmother laughed, too, because *her* daughter's laugh still made her.

"I shit a little when you were born," the old woman said. "With you, that was my first mistake."

Damn It, Damn It,
Damn It

Frances and her little brother Ben laughed at the old man because he said *chimbley* and *barfoot,* but they didn't laugh to his face. They wouldn't have hurt his feelings for a million dollars. They loved him. Well, they part loved him and part were scared of him. Maybe not scared exactly. More like impressed. It *impressed* them the way he could add numbers so quick in his head, and they loved his puzzling stories about terrapins making wagers with wild turkeys or bears throwing cobs at him out of the cornfield.

"Bear meat's good," he told them. "Tastes like hamburger."

"What even is a terrapin?" Ben asked, still with that funny syntax, even though he was eight. Frances was eleven, and her syntax was nearly perfect.

White people called the old man Godwin, and Black people called him Hopscotch for some reason Frances didn't know. In her own mind, she called him Godwin Pleasants, his whole lovely name. She and Ben had known him since they were babies and started coming to visit their grandmother, back when Gran still felt good and the Francis I flatware was still used at supper and hand-washed and dried and put away in its heavy felt-lined box every night. For years, Frances had thought she'd been named after the silver, or vice versa. She knew better now.

School was out for the summer, and Frances's mother, Helen, had sent the children to stay with their Aunt Delia at Fairview for a month so she wouldn't have to pay for camps while she and their father worked. Fairview was where Gran had grown up, a large two-story wooden house, two miles out from the town that was no longer a town, more a village with a stoplight and post office. Gran had moved away to marry and had retired here with Papa when Frances was small and Ben was not yet born. Now Gran and Papa were dead, and everybody was sad about it. When their mother had dropped them off on Saturday, she'd written out a long list of what Delia shouldn't allow them to do (a list Delia soon "misplaced"). Then she'd spent the afternoon scrubbing the kitchen while Delia leaned against the counter sipping a beer and talking about her on-again, off-again beau, Marshall.

"The problem with Marshall is that he thinks he needs to teach me to be a good person, and I'm pretty sure I am one already, more or less. That's just one of the areas of opinion where we differ, but I'd say it's an important one."

Helen motioned with her spray bottle for Delia to step aside so she could clean the counter.

"Maybe Marshall just doesn't understand how you can have all your books alphabetized by author but you can't find your car keys or remember to pay your bills on time."

"What does any of that have to do with goodness?"

Before Helen went home, she'd said to Frances, "I'm counting on you," and Frances had gotten the feeling that she was being left to take care of Aunt Delia as much as the other way around.

Since May, Delia had been staying at Fairview with only her yellow lab, Chip—short for Potato Chip, which was his color—and a boxy old television for company. She was supposed to be writing a book but wouldn't tell anybody what it was about. She'd lost weight since Gran died the year before and had gotten even worse about returning phone calls, which drove Helen crazy. Helen had been to Fairview half a dozen times to deal with Gran's estate—making the two-hour trip east from Raleigh so fast that she nearly always got a speeding ticket—and each time she'd come home more exasperated. Delia, she said, was practically no help at all. The big question was: what to do with Fairview? Their family had been living in the house since 1825, back when it was the big house of a plantation, and they'd been on that same piece of land for seventy-five years before that, and they'd never, never—not once—thrown away anything. That fact depressed Helen, who said one day they'd have to get rid of all that "old stuff" and "do something" about Fairview, but Frances closed her ears to that terrible idea. She loved Fairview. She never got tired of rooting around in all that "old stuff" in the drawers and blanket chests and closets. And the books! So many! On shelves in the high-ceilinged living room, in the den, and upstairs in the bedrooms—hundreds of books, many modern, others with leather covers, fine engravings, and flyleaves inscribed in fading ink by ancestors long dead.

But Fairview wasn't dead—far from it. There were wasps in the chimneys and, in the walls, mice, hiding from the snakes and the owls. Surrounding the house were six acres of grass, oaks, dogwoods, myrtles, azaleas, boxwoods, and the flowers Frances was learning to name: phlox and iris, hellebore and mock orange. In the woods bordering the yard on two sides lived deer and foxes and Godwin Pleasants's famous bears. At night, with the windows open (there was no central air), Frances could hear the frogs, cicadas, and crickets singing as she read herself to sleep atop the white cotton sheets, damp with humidity and thin with age. The whole place—house, yard, town, countryside—was bleak and beautiful, both, with a mystery in it that Frances wasn't sure thrilled her in quite the same way that other mysteries did. Ben said Fairview was haunted because their grandmother had died here, right in the big, carved tall-post bed Aunt Delia slept in downstairs. Frances told him he was being stupid, but out of his hearing she asked Delia didn't it creep her out, using the bed where her mother had died?

"No, honey, it makes me feel close to her."

Aunt Delia went on to say that if Fairview *was* haunted, Gran was only one ghost of many, and the least of the trouble. And then Frances had understood, dimly, that this was a place Delia herself was still trying to fathom.

IT HAD ONLY taken a few days for them to settle into a routine. First, breakfast in the little room behind the kitchen, prepared mostly by Frances while Ben set the table and Delia drank coffee and checked e-mail on her phone. After they ate, Delia sent them out to run around the yard before the heat became unbearable. Frances would ask didn't she need help with the dishes, but Delia always said no.

The kitchen was too small for more than one person to work in it, and anyway she liked seeing the children out the window while she loaded the dishwasher—it reminded her of when she and Helen used to play out there with their cousins. Back then Godwin Pleasants had tended the yard only on Saturdays, because during the week he went up to Norfolk to work in the shipyards. Back then he could do in one day at Fairview what it now took him all week to manage.

He was out there most mornings before they even got up. Sometimes his daughter Jolisa dropped him off; sometimes he walked. It was hard to believe he walked all that way, the way so long, and him so old, and the sun so hot, even early in the morning now that it was mid-June. He and Jolisa lived out a dusty road on the other side of town. You never went out that road that there wasn't a run-over black snake in the middle of it or a dead deer, one. Frances knew this because whenever she used to visit Fairview, every afternoon Gran would say, "Let's have a little tea party," like it was a spontaneous idea and not something she did every day. She'd boil water and put real tea leaves in a china teapot and get out the matching creamer and the sugar bowl—all Spode, from England. She'd count out enough cloth napkins and lay out slices of orange rat cheese and Ritz crackers on a plate, plus Little Debbies cut on the diagonal. She'd bring it all out with the cups and saucers and Francis I teaspoons rattling on the tray, which she set on the coffee table in the den, and while they had tea, she'd calmly tell Ben not to put his feet on the table or his finger up his nose and remind Frances that a lady never crossed her legs at the knee, only at the ankle.

But before the tea party could happen, they had to drive Godwin home. He sat with Gran up front, where they both smoked ferociously and without ceasing, the windows barely cracked, the ashtrays brimming. Once Ben got sick, and Gran said he must have inherited a weak stomach from their father. Nobody in her family had ever had such a thing as a weak stomach.

Mingled with the smoke was Gran's perfume, along with Godwin's smell of cut grass, gasoline, and leaf dust, and underneath all those smells lay whatever musk nature gave to grown people to advertise themselves, before work and habits laid other odors over their skin and hair. Frances used to wonder when she would develop a smell of her own; then one day she thought maybe she'd had one all along and was just too used to it to be able to identify it.

On these drives, Gran often fretted to Godwin that Aunt Delia would never settle down, jumping from thing to thing the way she did—jobs, cities, hobbies, men. As for Helen, she was just the opposite, always had been: she worked too hard, never stopped to smell the roses.

"Poor thing acts like she never even heard of a rose. I tell you, if my girls could blend their qualities, I'd have two perfect daughters instead of two that worry me to death."

"Shoot!" Godwin would say. "Don't tell me about daughters. I got twice as many as you got!"

Jolisa was the only one of Godwin's daughters who lived in the area; her three sisters had gone up north long ago. They came south only when there was a funeral or a wedding, always elegantly turned out and driving a new car or, sometimes, a new husband. Jolisa worked third shift at a plant twenty-two miles down the road, packaging sticky buns, the big ones with the gluey glaze smeared against the cellophane, always already stale when you bought them. She had two sons and was forever trying to get together enough money for doctors' bills and football shoes and bail.

Often Jolisa would just have gotten out of bed when they dropped off Godwin. "Poor Jolisa," Gran used to say, "I admire how she handles her lot in life, and she's always so *grateful*." Gran was always giving Jolisa things: food, when she had too much, or a silk blouse she was through with or a casserole dish that was perfectly good except for missing the lid.

When Gran offered sympathy for Jolisa's troubles with her boys, Jolisa would shrug and say, "I leave it all to the Master, 'cause he's got a plan."

Once Ben asked who the Master was, and Jolisa looked shocked.

"Why, *God*, sugar. Who else?"

Only in eastern North Carolina had the children ever heard God called the *Master*. That was not said by people at home in Raleigh. To Frances, the word conjured *disaster*, which it seemed Jolisa was always having one of, and Ben said all he could think about when he heard it was the *Master Blaster*, a powerful water gun he desired that shot high-pressure streams for spectacular distances and with which, he was certain, he could put out the eyes of the playground enemies who tormented him because he sucked at killball.

Now that Gran was gone, though, it fell to Aunt Delia to drive Godwin home. She didn't allow cigarettes in her car (even though she herself smoked sometimes, on the sly), and they didn't talk much, instead riding most of the way in silence, everybody staring out the windows at the peanut fields and pine trees and old tobacco barns falling in on themselves. Because he couldn't smoke, Godwin would drum his fingers on the armrest as they rode through town, with its several blocks of modest brick ranch houses and handful of big Victorians painted white, their shutters and gingerbread picked out in blue or green or black. They'd go past the white Baptist church, the gas station, and the grocery store, through the stoplight, and stop at the dinky post office to get the mail. The post office was near the defunct Episcopal church where all the babies in Frances's family had been christened and where her mother had been married and Gran had been funeralized, as Godwin said, the last service of any kind to have been held there.

After the post office, they'd ride out of town, past more fields and pine trees, past the Black Baptist church and its graveyard, past a collapsed house and a cluster of trailers, until they finally arrived at Godwin and Jolisa's place, a tan double-wide with a screened porch, beside which grew a clump of orange canna lilies taller than Ben.

All around the trailer, drifting in and out of piles, were parts from freezers, tractors, and other machines Godwin was working on. Parked alongside what he called a barn but looked to Frances like a shed was the sputtering Statesman riding mower Gran had let Godwin have for parts after he'd convinced her they needed a new mower at Fairview. "He cheated you," Frances's mother had grumbled, but Gran had just laughed and said she was glad for Godwin to have the old thing if it made him happy. He'd managed to keep it running and had even rigged up a kind of homemade plow dealie for it that he said would be useful in the unusual event of a real snow.

There'd been no call to use it yet, but he was proud of his plow. What was important was he'd made the thing. What was important was he knew how to make things. Aunt Delia said she envied him that. She could barely make supper, she said, and after a few days with her, Frances had found that to be true. Yards were Godwin Pleasants's sideline. What he was, if you asked him, was a mechanic. That had been his job up in the shipyard in Virginia, and that was why he still always wore his dark blue jumpsuit—he wanted people to see what he really was. The jumpsuit had once been a sturdy cotton canvas, but now it hung patched and slack behind where there was no meat on him. People came from every direction with their broken stuff, knowing he would only charge ten dollars for his time, no matter if the job took him a few minutes or all afternoon.

"It's like Daddy don't even know what year it is," Jolisa complained to Delia. "Got no idea what a dollar's worth in this day and age."

BEFORE FRANCES AND Ben had come to stay with Delia that summer, their mother had collected baby things from people at their church to take to Jolisa's new grandbaby. The baby's father was Jolisa's younger son, Edward. He would be a senior in the fall, talented enough at football that there was hope of a college scholarship, his life so far more promising than that of his older brother Davis, also a father, who had recently been jailed for larceny for the second time. He and a friend had burgled a store three towns over and made off with $247 and most of a hog.

"Can you believe it?" Frances overheard Delia tell Marshall on the phone. "Can you believe I'm living in a place where people steal hogs? Not even whole hogs. *Parts* of hogs!"

The first afternoon the children were there, when they drove Godwin home, Jolisa was sitting on the screened porch, a clear plastic shower cap over her curlers. She was smoking a cigarette and giving the baby a bottle of formula. The children ran up, eager to see the baby while Godwin helped Delia get the bags out of the car.

"Can I feed her?" Frances asked. She wanted to hold the baby, bad. She also wanted to get the baby away from that cigarette.

"Sugar, I wish you would."

Along with Godwin's wooden rocker and two fold-up lawn chairs, there was a white plastic shower chair, wide enough for Frances and Ben to share. They sat on it, and Jolisa put the baby in Frances's arms. She was about six weeks old now and tiny, only seven and a half pounds, Jolisa said. Ben leaned over and made a face, trying to get the baby to smile, and it was all Frances could do not to push him away. She already regarded the baby as more hers than his, on account of it was a girl.

"What's her name?" he asked.

"Radiance," Jolisa said. "Radiance Diane." She handed Frances the bottle and watched her wedge it between the baby's lips. She said it looked like Frances knew what she was doing.

Frances nodded. "I babysit back home."

"Yeah, like, twice," Ben said.

Oh, if she'd had a free hand... but she was too enchanted with Radiance to bother with Ben. It was just too good the way she was sucking and gazing up at Frances with that weird empty-eyed love only little, little babies could give.

Jolisa reached over to tip the bottle so Radiance didn't get a mouthful of air. Frances felt stupid for not knowing to do it herself. Godwin was coming through the screen door with two shopping bags. Nordstrom. Saks Fifth Avenue. When Delia had seen the bags, she said Helen must have been shopping at that big-ass fancy mall over near Durham, and Helen had told her, "I have to dress for my job. I can't just go around in sweatpants all day like you."

"Girls ain't nothing but trouble," Godwin grumbled.

"Aw, Daddy, you don't mean that."

"Like fun I don't." He set the bags down, took off his cap, and sank into his rocker with a sigh. Frances had noticed that his good nature always took a dip as soon as he got home and got comfortable. Seemed to her like it ought to be the opposite.

Jolisa appeared delighted. You could never have too many things for a baby; they dirtied them up so fast. She thanked Ben and Frances and Delia over and over, as though collecting it all had been their own idea, and Frances thought it a shame her mother was at her office, sitting in a meeting or writing her hundredth e-mail of the day, instead of hearing Jolisa's thanks. After all, she was the one who'd rounded up the stuff, then carefully sorted it, pulling out anything she deemed sorry. Poor people, she said, didn't want clothes with stains and broken zippers any more than well-off people did. She was the one who had gone out to Target and bought two of the biggest boxes of diapers they had and six large cans of formula. Jolisa and

Godwin had been such a help with Gran, she said; she wanted to do something nice for them.

"I know Terri will be excited," Jolisa said. "She's sleeping right now, poor thing. She had the clamps. Do you know what that is? That's a serious disease. It's nothing to fool with. And can you believe, sick as she was, her folks put her out? Because of the baby? Well, I said, Terri, sugar, you come on and stay with us, if you can stand us. So she did. I always wanted a girl so bad, and now the Master's sent me two!"

BACK HOME, FRANCES never thought of her family as rich. But when she came out to Fairview, she realized that they had been pretty wealthy once upon a time. There was the big house, and the Francis I, and the portraits of the greats and the great-greats, and the antique furniture, and the stories of relatives who had been in the colonial government or had written amusing letters while on trips to Europe. Nobody said much about slaves, but she knew they had been there, and it had only been in the past year or so that she'd begun to think about how different her family's life was from those of people like Godwin and Jolisa and the other people she saw down here, driving broken cars and standing around in front of the store, not having any work to go to.

Last fall, her mother had gotten her out of school early one Friday afternoon so they could come down and take Gran to the doctor. They'd been somewhere between Rocky Mount and Fairview when they'd gotten stuck behind a school bus gradually delivering children home. She'd been sharing her mother's annoyance at the bus's poky progress until she saw a boy get off the bus and run down a dirt driveway to a derelict wooden house she'd always assumed was abandoned. The boy had run right inside, and then she'd noticed for the first time the TV satellite dish on one corner of the sagging roof, and she realized he lived there.

"Did you see that?" she'd asked her mother.

"See what?"

ON THE PHONE, after the first two weeks had gone by, her mother asked what they'd been up to.

"Reading and watching movies and playing Scrabble. I wish you could see the baby. She's so cute. Jolisa always lets me feed her. Dumb old Ben, he thinks the baby recognizes him now because she looks at him when he says, 'Where's Ben?' but I just think any baby will look at you if you talk to it. Don't you?"

"Please tell me Ben's getting outside and not just watching TV."

"Ben is a hopeless case."

"Well, I hope Delia's not moping."

"Don't worry, Mama. We're taking care of each other."

It was true. They were. In the evenings, while Ben was busy with another blow-'em-up movie (he wasn't allowed to watch them at home), she and Delia would sit on Gran's tall-post bed and talk while Delia drank white wine and Chip lay on the cool bathroom floor and scratched the tile, running in his dreams. They played cards or painted their toenails; Frances ignored Delia's extravagant cheating, and Delia didn't get mad when Frances accidentally got polish on the bedspread. They talked about boys—Frances had just gotten over a crush, and Delia said she wasn't breaking up with Marshall, just slowing down. She'd gone up to Durham to see him twice since she'd moved out here, but she hadn't invited him to Fairview yet, though he kept hinting that he wanted to be asked.

"Trouble is, I just can't picture him here."

"You don't think he'd like it?"

"He'll say it's *interesting*, and I won't like the way he says it, and then we'll have a big fight. I just know it."

A few times, Aunt Delia cried. One time it was about missing Gran; once, it was Marshall; once, she said, it was merely existential.

ROUNDING THE BEND coming into town one afternoon, Frances spied up ahead a lone figure walking alongside the road. The man wore low-slung jeans and an oversized nylon Carolina Panthers shirt. Godwin leaned toward the windshield, squinting.

"That's my cousin Otis. He's got no business out walking with his bad leg."

The man's gait was indeed peculiar. The right leg didn't bend, as though it didn't have a joint, so he had to lean to the left and swing the right leg around to move forward.

Aunt Delia said, "Do you want me to offer him a ride, Godwin?"

"If you don't mind."

Delia slowed the car as they passed the man, then pulled over onto the verge. Tall weeds grabbed at the car's underbelly, tugging it to a stop. It was a small car, and when, a minute later, the stranger opened the door, Frances about had to sit on Ben to make room. He was too busy staring at the man to complain, though. The man wasn't tall, but he was built solid, and about his eyes was a grim wildness that terrified Frances when he turned toward her, baring his teeth, one of which was made of metal.

"Hello!" said Aunt Delia, her voice sounding the way a balloon looked when you accidentally let go of the string and it flew up into the sky. The man said nothing, and the echo of Delia's bright *hello* hung in the air, a sweet yellow dot against a blue sky, getting smaller as it went up into nothing.

They hadn't been back on the road two minutes when the man hit the back of Godwin's seat.

"Move your seat up, old man."

Aunt Delia told Godwin how to do it. When he'd adjusted it, he turned around halfway and said some folks' names to the man, asked how they were doing.

"Old man, I don't know what the fuck you're talking about."

For a moment, Frances heard only the tires rumbling over the asphalt, just as regular as if nothing was wrong.

"That's no way to talk in front of this lady and them children," Godwin said. "What's wrong with you?"

"Ain't shit wrong with me! What's wrong with you?"

The stranger popped Godwin in the back of the head.

"Ow! What'd you do that for?"

"'Cause I felt like it," said the man, and he hit Godwin again, harder this time, so that he cried out in real pain. He reached over the back seat, swatting, but the man grabbed his arm and twisted it so that Godwin yelled again.

"You let go of him!" Delia shouted, the car swerving as she turned to fuss.

"Watch out!" Frances cried. Delia steadied the car. Surprisingly, the man let go, and Godwin folded his hurt arm against his chest.

"You ain't Otis," he said.

"No shit!"

On the other side of Frances, Ben was shaking. She gave him a firm look and shook her head. He had to get it together! They were nearing the stoplight in town and might be able to jump out; since he was closest to the door, he needed to be ready to go.

But the man was saying, "Stop at the store."

Delia pulled into the parking lot. Seeing the handful of parked cars and three women talking by the ice cooler at the store's entrance, Frances thought maybe everything was going to be okay. The stranger fumbled his way out of the car, leaving the door wide open, and with his odd, stiff gait walked across the pavement and into the store. The three women watched him, watched Frances hurry to close and lock the door, watched as Delia careened out of the lot— and Frances watched them watching, sure she'd remember their faces forever because, in her mind, they somehow by their watching had saved her from an awful fate.

"WHAT'S THE MATTER with Little Man?" Jolisa nodded at Ben, who was still crying. She was wearing a royal blue dress and high heels. Her hair was fixed, and she had on gold earrings and a black-and-gold bead necklace. Frances had never seen her so fancy before. Any other day she would have asked what the occasion was, but now she said nothing.

"We had a bit of a scare on the way here," Aunt Delia said, hugging Ben to her side.

"We give Arvell James a ride," Godwin said.

Jolisa's face! If everybody hadn't been so upset, Frances would've laughed.

"I thought it was Cousin Otis," Godwin said. He lit a cigarette.

"That crackhead don't even look like Otis! You must need new glasses."

Jolisa frowned at Delia and Frances, scandalized that they hadn't been able to recognize that a man as rough as Arvell James couldn't possibly be her cousin.

"They got the same walk," Godwin protested.

Jolisa held up her hand to show that she couldn't take him right then, not at all.

She said, "Why don't you go get Little Man a Coke?"

As soon as Godwin went inside, Delia said in a low voice, "Don't be too hard on him. He's pretty shaken up."

"That man hit him," Frances said.

"Twice," Ben sniffed.

"Arvell James! I would no more give him a ride . . . Steals anything that's not nailed down, and just as soon knock you in the head as look at you. All them Jameses the same way. His grandmother that raised him poisoned two husbands. Did you know that? And I could tell you worse besides, but it's not fit for children to hear."

Jolisa sat on one of the lawn chairs, produced a tissue from her pocket, pulled Ben over to her, and wiped his face.

She said, "Don't you be ashamed. I'd have cried, too, if Arvell James got in my car."

Godwin came out with Cokes and handed them around.

"Did Arvell hurt you, Daddy?"

Frances had never seen Jolisa's face look so hard. The Jolisa she knew was soft, smiling; she wore sweatpants and curlers, offered cookies, let everything roll off her. This Jolisa, decked in a jewel-colored dress and makeup and gold beads, was different. She had a power to her.

When he said nothing, she asked again.

"Did he hurt you?"

"Wrenched my arm, that's all. Give me a headache. If I could've got a good angle on him, I would've laid him out."

"Oh, please, Daddy, you're three times his age, and anyway, you know Arvell James ain't nobody to fool with."

"Well, if I see him around this place, he's going to be full of lead."

Jolisa blew out a derisive puff of air. "Talking big."

"Don't you think we ought to call the police?" Delia said. "Report that man for assault?"

Jolisa said, "And just what do you think they're going to do?"

THE LADY DELIA talked to at the police station said they already knew Arvell James was a bad character. What had Delia been thinking, picking up somebody like that? Godwin Pleasants could press charges if he wanted to, but that seemed unlikely, given his own run-ins with the law, and besides no judge was going to bother with a case of one Black man hitting another one.

Frances heard it all because the only way Aunt Delia could get cell reception at Fairview was to put on the speaker and hold the phone up to the back window in the breakfast room and holler at it.

"I swear, these people down here." She trailed off then, taking a piece of the orange Frances was peeling, but she didn't have to say any more for Frances to get the point. Frances knew perfectly well what a bigot was and that it was very wrong to be one. She had learned all about that at school and also at home where, every MLK day, her father made her and Ben watch Dr. King's "I Have a Dream" speech on YouTube. Her mother, at Frances's Girl Scout meetings, was careful when necessary to say "African American" so as to respect the two dark-skinned girls in the group, who were Indian, not Native American, but Indian meaning their parents were from India or maybe their grandparents. Frances wasn't sure which. Not that her mother called *them* "African American," but she seemed to think it important to use careful terminology in *front* of them. At home, her mother usually just said "Black" because that was what she had grown up with, she said, and it was hard to change.

"It's okay," Frances told her, "the Black kids at my school still say Black. You just can't say stuff like '*the* Blacks' or say that only Black people like this and only white people like that, because then you're being racist."

It was a lot to think about, once you really stopped to think.

At supper, Ben pushed his spaghetti around and said, "What if that man comes to *get* us?"

Aunt Delia patted his shoulder and pretended it wasn't what all of them had been thinking all day.

"Oh, honey, don't worry about that. He doesn't care about us, and besides, he doesn't even know where we live."

That satisfied Ben, but Frances knew that anybody in the one-stoplight town could guess who they were and where they stayed. When she lay in bed later, she thought of all the ways Arvell James, high on drugs and enraged by circumstance, could *get* them. For once, she was glad to be sharing the room with Ben, who insisted on keeping the light on when he lay down in the twin bed across from her. From the way he flopped and huffed, trying to settle himself, she could tell he wasn't asleep yet, but at least he'd stopped talking. She didn't know how Aunt Delia could sleep downstairs with her windows open. If it weren't so hot, Frances would close the windows in their room. After all, it was possible Arvell James had a ladder. Oh, well, at least Chip would bark if anybody came prowling around, and that might give them time to lock themselves in the bathroom.

For the first time in her memory, the noise of the night creatures outside seemed more menace than comfort. For the first time, she considered how many thousands of jumping, scuttling creatures it took to make such a big pervasive noise. She went over and turned up the box fan as high as it would go.

THE NEXT DAY was Sunday, so they didn't expect Godwin, but when he didn't come on Monday or Tuesday, Frances began to worry. She asked why didn't Aunt Delia call him. Delia said he'd turn up when he was ready.

That evening, after supper, the house phone rang. The noise surprised Frances—she hadn't known the faded yellow push-button phone hanging on the kitchen wall still worked. Taped up next to it was a list of numbers written in Gran's hand, half of them crossed out because the people had died. The phone kept ringing, and Frances realized she'd have to answer it because Delia, who favored long hot baths even in the summer, was in the tub.

At first she didn't understand that it was Godwin Pleasants calling. His voice sounded thick, as though he had a mouthful of something he couldn't dislodge. She thought he was saying for her to get her mama, and she tried to remind him that her mother was in Raleigh. Whatever he said next made no sense, and after that, whenever she spoke, there would be a long silence until he would say, "Miss Delia? It's Godwin," and start rambling again.

By and by, Frances understood that he thought *she* was Delia and that he'd forgotten Gran was dead and wanted to talk to her so he could tell her that he needed some money. Frances wondered how that could be since he'd just been paid on Saturday. She'd seen Aunt Delia give him the twenties—she didn't know how many because he'd hastily put them in his pocket without counting, the way he always did, the whole embarrassed sleight of hand between them like a magic trick they performed together.

"Just ten dollars," he was begging. "Please."

He sounded so distant, like a man down a well, hollering up toward a daylight he could barely see.

"Or a sandwich? If I could just get a sandwich. Jolisa put me out. She tried to kill me. Pushed me down. Think I broke my foot. Oh, it hurts so bad."

Frances was alarmed that he was telling her these things. What could she do, a little girl? It was like talking to a stranger instead of a person she'd known all her life.

"Hold on," she said. "Let me find Aunt Delia."

She put the receiver down on the counter, went out of the kitchen, through the hall, past Ben on the couch in the den where he was watching an explosion on TV, then on through the dark living room they rarely used, with its shrouded, slipcovered shapes and curtains always drawn against the summer sun, through the office to Aunt Delia's room, where a lamp burned on Gran's dressing table. Chip lay on the floor in front of the bathroom, and when Frances reached over him to knock on the six-paneled door, he opened one brown eye but didn't move.

"Godwin's on the phone. He sounds weird. I think he might be sick."

Behind the door, Aunt Delia said, "Honey, he's all right. Just tell him I'll talk to him later."

Frances hesitated, then crossed the house again. The phone was bleating on the counter. There was nothing for her to do but hang up, too. She went into the den to watch TV with Ben. It made her so mad, all these things grown people let swirl in the air, like smoke, and wouldn't explain. Even Delia, who Frances's mother said didn't have a practical bone in her body, was in on things Frances wasn't allowed to know. How was that fair? One day Frances was going to know everything there was to know about everything, and people wouldn't be able to hide things from her all the time, damn it. She had developed a habit of thinking *damn it* to herself whenever grown-ups irritated her, which, now that she was eleven, was happening more and more, so that her mind was like a caged bird that said *damn it, damn it, damn it* all damn day, and she couldn't give it enough crackers to shut it up.

Look at Ben, sitting there with his mouth hanging open, watching that stupid television. He had forgotten all about Arvell James, all about Godwin Pleasants. He just wanted to see things on fire. Boys.

Frances wandered into the living room and turned on the floor lamp next to the piano, which was a grand but didn't sound it. The mildewed felt inside gave off a musty smell, and the bench creaked like it would disintegrate when she sat on it, but she enjoyed playing. Inside the bench was sheet music from the 1920s and '30s that had belonged to Gran's grandmother, all of it too difficult for Frances, but she liked to look at the covers. She still remembered her last two recital pieces, one called "Skipping Along," the other a simple arrangement of "Für Elise." She was playing that a second time when Delia passed by in her green bathrobe, toweling her hair, and had started the tune yet again when Delia came back, holding a glass and an ice bucket with a wine bottle in it. She stood to listen and, when Frances was done, said she played nicely.

"No, I don't."

"Well, you're improving. That's the main thing. You want to come hang out in my room?"

"It's Gran's room," Frances said, just to be ornery, but when Delia walked away, she followed. Delia propped up against the pillows and put lotion on her arms while Frances sat at the foot of the bed and shuffled a deck of cards. The picture on the back was a cancan dancer, showing her leg. Frances had found the cards way at the back of a drawer, along with a dried-up lipstick redder than blood and a lighter that had run out of fluid.

"I thought you cared about Godwin. Why didn't you come to the phone?"

"Because he never calls at night unless he's drunk."

"Okay..." Frances said, pulling at one of the white fluff balls on the chenille bedspread, "but you're drinking."

"There's a difference between my glass of wine or three and the way Godwin drinks."

Frances dealt, and they played a hand without talking. It was just War they were playing, not a thinking kind of game, but still you couldn't really do conversation because you had to keep up the pace. Frances won, then gathered all the cards and shuffled again.

Delia said, "I remember one time, when I was about your age, I was riding home on the school bus and these kids called this sweet little boy the N word. You know what that is?"

Frances nodded.

"Well, I screamed at those kids to quit. I mean, I really went crazy, screaming at them. And then when the little boy got off the bus, I did, too, even though it wasn't my stop. He didn't say anything to me, but I walked behind him until I was sure he was home safe."

"That was good."

"At the time, I thought I was doing a really good, brave thing, but then later I wondered if maybe I'd just embarrassed him. What if he thought I was following him because I was going to be mean to him, too? Maybe I scared him."

"He knew you were nice. Everybody knows you're nice."

Frances wished her aunt would just pick up her cards and play, but she wasn't paying attention to the game anymore.

"You're sweet," Delia said. "But see, when I think about it now, I realize maybe I wasn't thinking of him. Maybe I just wanted to feel like I was being good. Patting myself on the back."

"But you *are* a good person."

Delia poured herself another glass of wine and stared across the room at the old photographs of Gran's family and the cold fireplace.

"Think what it would be like," she said, "to be as smart as Godwin and to live in a place like this all your life, where people still do things the old ways."

"Why doesn't he leave here, then?"

"Probably one of the usual things that stops people leaving a place. Money? Love? Inertia? Fear?"

"Fear of what?"

"Anything? Everything?"

Delia squirted lotion into her hand and rubbed it onto Frances's right foot, kneading gently. After a few minutes, Frances felt so relaxed she had to close her eyes.

"I was afraid of Arvell James."

"I know. Me, too. Marshall says we're all racists. He says we learn it before we ever have a choice, and by the time we're able to make a choice, it's too late. It's already in you. But if I press him and say, so you're a racist, too, he'll just say, 'We all are, on some level.' Thing is, he *says* all that stuff about everybody being racist, but deep down he doesn't believe *he* is. He thinks that if he worries about things like whether it's okay for white people to laugh at Black comedians' jokes about other Black people, then he's fighting the power, you know? But what's he doing, really?"

Frances put the cards aside and lay down. She felt so tired. Aunt Delia started on her left foot.

"I wasn't scared of that man because he was Black," Frances said. "He just—had a scary look."

She didn't know how to explain to Delia what scared her about the stranger. She didn't *think* it was his color. It wasn't his obvious strength or the metal tooth or even the mean things he did. What scared her was the way he didn't seem to see any of them, as though his eyes were instruments not for taking in the unspeakable world but for broadcasting what he thought of it.

"Godwin's cousin or not," Delia said, "I shouldn't have picked him up. He was a man I didn't know. And I was a woman with children in the car. That's what your mother would say."

"Oh, I won't tell her," Frances said sleepily. "But Ben will."

JOLISA CAME BY with a package of sticky buns to thank them for the baby clothes. She wouldn't get out of the car because Chip was running around barking. While Delia was trying to catch him to put him in the house, Jolisa rolled down the windows and handed the sticky buns to Ben. He grinned because he was the only one who liked them and knew he'd get to eat them all.

Behind Jolisa, Radiance was buckled into her car seat, wearing a pink romper with a cupcake on it. Sitting on the swirled white icing were two yellow kittens, kissing, and surrounding them were tiny white hearts, shooting off in every direction like sparks.

Frances stared into the brown, depthless eyes that were studying her. All morning she'd been thinking about what Delia had said last night and wondering if she'd been scared of Arvell James *before* he'd hit Godwin or only after. It seemed very important to try to figure that out.

Worse, she was still afraid, and the most likely reason she could come up with was one she didn't like at all: maybe she was always afraid.

How long did a baby like Radiance have in the world before she began to be afraid, too? How long before she found out about people like Frances? Frances didn't want to be a person who could be afraid of Arvell James before she knew he *was* Arvell James, before she even knew there was such a thing, such a person as Arvell James. She stared harder into the baby's eyes and searched her heart for love. It didn't take her long to find it. There it was, running all around her insides, warm and syrupy, but after a minute she thought sadly that her little test wasn't good enough. Anybody could love a baby, any kind.

THAT FALL, AFTER Frances and Ben had been back in school a month or so, their mother brought them out to Fairview for a weekend visit. Godwin Pleasants had turned up by then and was soberly dealing with the fallen leaves on the place, the long, bent teeth of his rake scratching, scratching, all day long.

Mrs. DeVry, Hanging Out the Wash
or What Kind of Pie, Mrs. DeVry?

———

When my father was a boy during World War II, he says, he was at the movies with his father one evening. The newsreel had just finished and the first chords of the feature's soundtrack had begun when the usher came down the aisle, shining his flashlight and saying my grandfather's name. They followed him into the lobby where a policeman in uniform was waiting, eating popcorn out of a bag. My father was afraid.

"I thought Daddy was being arrested," he says.

But instead the policeman said there had been an accident, and they got in my grandfather's car and followed the policeman to the hospital, the same one where I was born, thirty years later, in a wing not then built. My father waited with the policeman while my grandfather disappeared down a hallway with a nurse. The policeman, still eating his popcorn between drags on a cigarette, talked to my father about school and baseball and a time he'd seen a man in a traveling show shoot sixteen peach cans off a woman's outstretched arms with a .22 pistol. Afterward, she didn't have a scratch on her, and each can had a perfect hole in it, right through the picture of the halved peach on the label, right where the pit would have been.

"Don't that beat all?" said the policeman.

My father said that it did.

"What was the feature tonight, son? I've seen 'em all. I can tell you if you ought to be sorry you missed it."

My father told him the name of the picture, which, all these years later, he says he can't remember.

"And what did the policeman say about it?" I asked.

"I don't know what he was going to say because that's when Daddy came out holding Granny's blue pocketbook, and I knew."

THEY WENT THE next day and looked at the stretch of dirt alongside the railroad track where my great-grandmother had been struck down at dusk by a freight train headed north. My grandfather paced up and down for what seemed to my father an hour, studying the ground, his hands in his pockets.

"I don't know if he was looking for something of hers or if he was trying to find the exact spot where she died—a bloodstain or an indentation in the dirt, something like that. He never said a word. He'd walk down the track twenty or thirty yards, and then he'd come on back and walk up the track twenty or thirty yards. I can't tell you how many times. I stood by the car—he had a '38 Ford then—and I kept my eyes peeled for a train. I was petrified he was going to get run over, just like Granny."

"Did he find anything?"

"No. After a while, he came back to the car, and we went home, and a day or two later, we had a funeral."

"What year was that?"

"1944. I was seven."

About Walker's age. Walker, my son, is eight. He's with me half the time and with his father and stepmother the rest. My parents are very upset by this division, but to me it seems about right. I'm only able to be a good mother about half the time. I try to make sure it's on the days Walker is with me. I try to make sure there's healthy food in the house; I shower and put on real clothes; I pick up after the dog in the backyard so that Walker can run around out there if he wants to, but he never does. Like me, he'd rather sit on the sofa together, reading or watching a movie. He likes being in the house.

It's a nice, two-story house with wood floors, a butler's pantry we turned into a breakfast nook, and a stained-glass window on the stair landing, a funny window with assorted garnet and emerald and amber and violet panes, and in the middle of it, a clear pane with a picture of a hedgehog who doesn't look too bright. That window was why I wanted the house—too big for us even when we bought it—a rambly old house just right for a couple and two or three children and the occasional overnight company and a big party once a year that all your friends count on being invited to. I still love it and don't plan to move, even though it's too much for me and Walker and one geriatric dog that can't make it up the stairs anymore. When something breaks or stops working—and something always does—it just has to stay that way until my father finds a Saturday when he can come over and take care of it.

When he came a few months ago to rehang the screen door, he brought a bunch of boxes in from his truck and put them in the nearly empty back room that had been my ex-husband's home office.

"What's all this, Dad?"

"What's all this? What's all this? *This*, young lady, is the train."

"*The* train?"

"*My* train. The train my father put together for me when I was a boy."

"The train Joanna and I were never allowed to play with because we were girls?"

"Your grandfather asked you and your sister a hundred times if you wanted to play with it, and you always said no."

That's not the way I remember it, but all I said was, "Do you think it still runs?"

"I'll make it run, by God."

He went back out to his truck and brought in this giant piece of plywood. Then another one. Then sawhorses. I saw that it was going to be a whole thing. A project. My mother was going to be calling Saturday afternoons when it started to get dark, wanting to know if my father was ever coming home. Joanna was going to pretend to feel sorry for me, but really she would be jealous the train had come to live at my house, and I would like it.

"And you won't be mad if Walker messes it up? Or me?"

He leaned the plywood against the wall, careful not to scratch the paint. Took my hands, clasped them together, looked me in the eye as he kissed my fingertips.

"Butterbean," he said, "I trust you."

WHEN WE USED to visit our grandparents, Joanna and I would sneak up to the attic to see the train. It was set up on a huge table, maybe ten by fourteen feet, that was covered with nubby dark green turf. There were hills and a silver lake, clumps of forest and a farm out from town with belted cows, speckled chickens, and a farmhand in overalls carrying a bucket of slop to the pigs. In the town was a depot and a main street with shops, a brick schoolhouse with a bell, a steepled white church. The clock at the top of the courthouse really ran, and out front, in a gazebo, young lovers kissed while kids ate tiny ice cream cones on a park bench. There was a family strolling across the street while a policeman stopped the traffic, five old-fashioned cars that looked like they'd be awful hot to ride in in the summertime.

Down the street was a black Scottie dog wearing a red collar and standing inside a white picket fence. The fence enclosed a yellow house and a yard where a brown-haired woman in a green dress and white apron was hanging out her wash, a wee basket of clothes at her feet. What was she thinking about, I used to wonder. What was it like in her little yellow house? I was dying to get in there and see. Did she have a pie in the oven? What kind? Was there a baby napping in a crib upstairs, all flush cheeked and sweet, with its diapered butt up in the air? Was there, on the woman's kitchen table, a miniscule book that she was eager to get back to reading before the baby woke up?

I found her the other day. It wasn't a Walker day, and it wasn't a work day, and I was aimless. I'd eaten leftover Thai curry, two cookies, and eight grapes for breakfast, and I was wandering around the house nursing my coffee, feeling sorry for myself for no reason I could put my finger on. I went into the train room, now nearly filled by the plywood table my dad had set up. The original layout from my grandparents' attic had been thrown out long ago, so Dad was building a new one. While I was running errands one afternoon, he and Walker had unpacked the train cars and buildings and itty-bitty people and lined them up on the shelves that used to hold my husband's books.

My god, I'd forgotten how tiny the people were. I picked up the woman in the green dress and white apron. She's only an inch tall and feels like a wooden matchstick between my fingers. When I was a child, I called her Mrs. DeVry. I had a little rhyme.

Oh Mrs. DeVry, why do you cry, out by your line all day?

It's Mr. DeVry, he said goodbye, off to the war far away.

WHEN MY DAD showed Walker how everything was going to be laid out on the table, he shook his head and said he didn't want it "all old school."

"This is going to be the Mythology Express, Grandpa. Like, Mount Olympus will be over here in this corner, and the River Styx will be here, and Hades will be over here, with like—we can make some flames, you know, out of red and orange paper—and over here will be Delphi with a temple where people can get off the train and consult the oracle. Won't that be awesome?"

Dad looked stunned, as he so often does when Walker speaks, and then he clapped Walker on the shoulder and said, "Well, Applejack, sounds like we better get busy."

So we started building a world, the three of us. I painted columns for the temple, while Dad and Walker made mountains out of papier-mâché. We had the windows open and some Wilson Pickett on, and it was as fine a Saturday as I ever expect to spend.

DAD AND I were disappointed, though, about the village being cast aside. I pleaded our case with Walker. I said there had to be a place where the mortals could live.

"Why do we even need mortals?" he asked.

"Because otherwise the gods wouldn't have anybody to lord over."

He said that was a good point and let us put the village at the far end of the table, more tightly clustered than it was in the old days, but at least it's there, and Mrs. DeVry is back at the line, hanging out her wash. She has begun writing poems at her kitchen table in her spare time, so now I call her Mrs. Sylvia Anne DeVry, after Plath and Sexton, even though I know Mrs. DeVry will never be as accomplished as they were. But then you can't expect that—she hasn't had their advantages in life, now has she?

The other day, I sent Mrs. Sylvia Anne DeVry to the oracle. I walked her up the temple steps and stood her at the top, facing the door, and she told the oracle all about herself, a thing Walker would not sanction.

"Mom! People don't tell the oracle stuff—the oracle tells *them.* They can just ask one question—that's all!"

But Mrs. Sylvia Anne DeVry can't avoid the confessional impulse. It's too much a part of her nature. So she told the oracle all about her infidelities and her temper tantrums and the problems she has at her job that she had to get after her husband came back from wartime France a distant, ruined man. She told the oracle that once she even considered going down to the tracks and flinging herself on them, like the woman in the fat book sitting on her kitchen table, but of course she didn't because how could a woman leave her children like that? Mrs. DeVry could never do that to her sweet baby, at home napping with his bottom in the air.

And the Oracle sayeth, with serious impatience, "I have many people to see, Mrs. DeVry. What is your question?"

Mrs. DeVry said, "What should my question be?"

And the Oracle sayeth, "Come back tomorrow."

I WONDER ABOUT that night when my great-grandmother was run down by that freight headed north. What was the train carrying? Supplies for the war effort? What was she doing out there, walking at dusk not far from the small house where she lived, a widow all alone? Was she crossing the tracks to visit a friend or maybe go to a store where she could buy Lucky Strikes or a can of beans? How did her blue pocketbook survive the accident, her wallet and handkerchief and unbroken glasses in a case, all tucked inside, all perfectly intact? Had her purse been thrown clear when she was struck by the train? Or did she set it down before walking onto the track?

And why, when my father came out into the bright lobby of the Varsity Theater and saw the policeman standing there, did he think his father had done something wrong and was being arrested? What had they just seen on the newsreel, and would the movie they were about to watch have been enough to put that war news out of their minds for an hour or two? How could that policeman so blithely eat popcorn while he delivered such terrible, life-changing information?

And why did my grandfather keep that train set up in the attic until he died, a very old man, never having let my father take away what was rightfully his? Why did my grandfather sit up there alone and watch the train run round and round, winding through the hills and over the lake, past the farm and through the town, right by the yellow house where a pie is baking and a baby is napping and Mrs. Sylvia Anne DeVry, hanging out the wash, hears the train and mistakes it for the sound of a change coming?

Acknowledgments

The following stories were previously published:

"At the Arrowhead," *Southern Review* (Autumn 2018)

"Cleopatra's Needle," *Chelsea*, no. 76 (Summer 2004)

"Hot Lesbian Vampire Magic School," failbetter.com, 2015, issue 56

"Flown," *Cincinnati Review*, vol. 19, no. 2 (Fall 2022)

"Delta Foxtrot," *Greensboro Review*, no. 97 (Spring 2015)

"Tooth," *Arts and Letters: Journal of Contemporary Culture*, issue 8 (Fall 2002). Reprinted in *The Sincerest Form of Flattery: Contemporary Women Writers on Forerunners in Fiction*, edited by Jacqueline Kolosov and Kirsten Sundberg Lunstrum (Lewiston, ID: Lewis-Clark Press, 2008).

"Et tu, Miss Jones?" *Literary Matters*, vol. 15, no. 1 (Fall 2022)

"The Woman Who Did Things Wrong," *Copper Nickel*, no. 36 (Spring 2023)

"Damn It, Damn It, Damn It," *Alaska Quarterly Review*, vol. 35, nos. 1 & 2 (Summer/Fall 2018)

"Mrs. DeVry Hanging Out the Wash" appeared as "Mrs. DeVry, Why Do You Cry?" in *Southern Cultures*, vol. 22, no. 3 (Fall 2016)

This collection was a long time in the making, and I'm grateful to more folks than I can name for their help and support over the years.

Enormous thanks to my brilliant agent Maggie Cooper at Aevitas Creative Management, as well as to the dedicated folks at Blair, especially Robin Miura, Lynn York, and Arielle Hebert.

Thank you to the editors who first published these stories: Ronald Spatz (*Alaska Quarterly Review*); Martin Lammon and Kellie Wells (*Arts and Letters*); Alfredo de Palchi and Robert McPhillips (*Chelsea*); Michael Griffith and Lisa Ampleman (*Cincinnati Review*); Wayne Miller and Joanna Luloff (*Copper Nickel*); Thom Didato (*failbetter*); Terry Kennedy, Jim Minick, and Jim Clark (*Greensboro Review*); Joanna Pearson and Ryan Wilson (*Literary Matters*); Ayse Erginer, Patrick Horn, and Emily Wallace (*Southern Cultures*); Garrett Hazelwood, Sacha Idell, and Jessica Faust (*Southern Review*).

Thank you to those who read early drafts and offered valuable feedback and encouragement, particularly Elizabeth Evitts Dickinson, Bryan Giemza, Dorothy Hans, Margot Livesey, Glenn Perkins, Rachel Richardson, Nina Riggs, Amy Rowland, Laura Schmitt, and Stephanie Whetstone.

Thank you to Holly Goddard Jones, Gwen Kirby, Joanna Pearson, and Kevin Wilson for taking time out of very busy schedules to read the manuscript and write blurbs that make my head swell.

Thank you to the Arts Council of Greater Greensboro, the Cuttyhunk Island Residency, the Sewanee Writers' Conference, the Virginia Center for Creative Arts, and the Weymouth Center for the Arts and Humanities for supporting my work.

Thank you to my UNC Chapel Hill colleagues and students for continuing to teach me about writing—and for making it fun to come to school.

Thank you to my friends and family for your camaraderie, patience, help, and love.

And thanks, most of all, to Glenn and Theo for our life together.